My Wife Is A Goblin Slayer

M Safee

Published by M Safee, 2023.

Also by M Safee

The Forgotten Whisper
Love Lies Secrecy
My Wife Is A Goblin Slayer

Table of Contents

To My Dearest Wife,

In the pages of our lives, you are the most cherished chapter. This dedication is a testament to the boundless love, strength, and joy you bring into my world every day. Through life's trials and triumphs, we stand together, united by a love that knows no bounds. Your presence is a beacon of light, guiding me through every storm. With you by my side, life's adventures are filled with laughter, compassion, and unwavering support. You are the truest partner and the most beautiful soul I have ever known. With this dedication, I express my deepest gratitude for the gift of your love and for the promise of a future filled with endless love and happiness. I am forever blessed to call you my wife.

With all my love, M Safee

My wife is a goblin slayer
M SAFEE

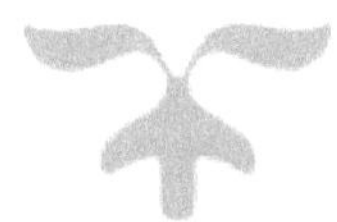

Chapter 1 Unveiling the Mystery

The downpour fell tirelessly, pattering against the windows of Michael Craig's Victorian home, as though the sky sobbed pair with the shadows that stuck to his spirit. It was a night shrouded in a demeanor of despairing, where the heaviness of the world appeared to settle upon his shoulders. Looking for comfort in the isolation of his loft, he wandered into the neglected openings of his past, expecting to find relief from the whirlwind that seethed inside him.

In the midst of the residue covered relics and failed to remember recollections, Michael coincidentally found an obsolete wooden chest, settled in the midst of the neglected corners of the upper room. His interest, ever the immovable friend, constrained him to examine its items. As he lifted the top, the fragrance old enough and insider facts drifted through the air, stirring his detects.

Settled inside the chest was a collection, its cover worn and endured by the progression of time. Michael cautiously opened the pages, uncovering a sepia-conditioned embroidery of recollections. Each photo was a depiction frozen in time, catching passing snapshots of bliss, love, and distress. His look settled upon a picture that appeared to radiate an odd atmosphere — a picture of his adored spouse, Sarah.

In this specific photo, Sarah's eyes glinted with a steadfast assurance, her fragile hands firmly getting a handle on a particular edge. Michael's foreheads wrinkled in disarray. How had he never seen this photo? What was the significance behind this baffling depiction? His psyche started to wind around an embroidery of inquiries, and an unwavering interest ignited inside his chest.

Driven by a voracious requirement for replies, Michael set out to wander into the profundities of his significant other's secret. He tried to disentangle the strands of her life that stayed disguised, taken cover behind the shroud of time and mystery. For he understood that, chasing truth, he gambled finding parts of his significant other that he never comprehended existed.

Subsequently, shrouded in the dimness of the evening, Michael set out on his stealthy investigation. He noticed Sarah's comings and goings, her collaborations with the world, with newly discovered watchfulness. Every day, he shadowed her strides, his eyes ever vigilant, anxious to strip away the layers of her reality, to fathom reality that lay covered underneath her cryptic exterior.

It was on a twilight night, when the shadows hit the dance floor with an unpleasant charm, that Michael coincidentally found a disclosure that opposed all explanation. Following Sarah through the tangled roads of London, he watched in wonder as she shed her delicate pretense, changing into a fearless fighter — a Troll Slayer. The acknowledgment hit him with the power of a thunderclap, and a bunch of feelings flooded inside him.

With an extraordinary elegance, Sarah traveled through the obscured back streets, her means directed by an inconspicuous power. Her figure was enveloped by a shroud of secret, as she faced odd animals that prowled in the evening — trolls with vindictive goal. In her grasp, she used the exceptional sharp edge from the photo, its flickering steel slicing through the haziness like an encouraging sign.

Michael's heart beat in his chest as he saw this secret fight, his psyche catching to fathom reality that unfurled before his eyes. How had his cherished Sarah become entangled in this hazardous presence? What impulse drove her to take part in this ceaseless conflict against the animals of dimness? An ensemble of dread, esteem, and disarray whirled inside him, making a turbulent tempest.

A large number of evenings, Michael got back to the safe-haven of their home, his brain burning with unanswered inquiries, his spirit wrestling with the heaviness of this recently discovered information. The lady he had vowed his life to, the lady whose profundities he assumed he had plumbed, had changed into a mystery — a many-sided puzzle not entirely set in stone to unravel, piece by tricky piece.

As the days seeped into evenings, and evenings into days, the gap between them developed, augmenting with each implicit truth. Sarah, detecting the break that had shaped, started to pull out into herself, her eyes hidden with a glint of culpability and trepidation. Maybe she also had detected the approaching tempest that took steps to immerse their lives.

One night, as Michael sat in their review, his psyche distracted with the riddle that had consumed him, Sarah went into the room. Her presence mixed the air, loaded down with a feeling of both fear and yearning. The candlelight cast a delicate shine upon her elements, enlightening the heap feelings that moved inside her eyes.

"Michael," she started, her voice touched with weakness, "there is something I should admit — a reality that has troubled my spirit for a really long time."

Michael's look locked with hers, his heart hurting for the association that had immediately melted away. He enticed her forward, his voice delicate yet weighty with expectation.

"Please tell me, my dear Sarah. Reveal the mysteries that exist in you, and let us face them together."

A quake flowed through her thin edge as she moved forward, her voice a murmur that conveyed the heaviness that could only be described as epic. "I'm a Troll Slayer, Michael," she uncovered, her voice shaking with a combination of dread and conviction. "It is a mantle I have borne, an obligation I have carried to shield the guiltless from the repulsions that sneak in the shadows."

The words lingered palpably, suspended between them, as reality settled inside Michael's being. The disclosure crashed over him like a violent wave, taking steps to immerse his detects. His brain hustled to accommodate the lady he had known — the delicate, cherishing soul — with this freshly discovered way of life as a fighter in a fight against the murkiness.

Tears welled in Sarah's eyes as she observed Michael's befuddled articulation, the heaviness of her admission bearing vigorously upon her. "I get it assuming this disclosure makes a huge difference, Michael," she mumbled, her voice bound with a propensity of torment. "Yet, I beseech you to see past the cover that different us. To see the adoration that has bound us, even as my obligation has driven me down this tricky way."

Michael's heart expanded inside him, a downpour of feelings flowing through his veins. At that time, he comprehended that their adoration was no simple string to be cut off by the disclosures of a solitary evening. It was an embroidery woven after some time, braced by the hardships they had endured together.

"My dear Sarah," he murmured, his voice a delicate stroke against the turbulent evening, "your admission doesn't reduce the adoration I bear for you. Regardless, it enlightens the profundities of your personality, the exceptional lengths to which you will go to safeguard those you hold dear. Allow me to remain close by, not as a simple eyewitness, but rather as your unflinching partner in this wild fight against the powers that try to desolate our reality."

A promising sign flashed inside Sarah's eyes as she ventured nearer, their spirits adjusting in a snapshot of significant comprehension. They stood, joined even with the riddle that had taken steps to destroy them. Furthermore, as the downpour kept on falling, washing away the leftovers of uncertainty and vulnerability, they promised to defy the shadows together — connected at the hip.

Much to their dismay that their mission for truth would divulge an evil embroidery of wrongdoing, secret, and experience that would challenge their affection, light their spirits, and perpetually change the direction of their lives.

Chapter 2: Love at First Sight

I t was 1887, when the world overflowed with both miracle and vulnerability. In the core of London, in the midst of the clamoring roads and foggy gleam of gas lights, a youthful Michael Craig ended up charmed by the energy of life and the boundless conceivable outcomes it held. It was during this lively age that destiny would interweave his way with that of Sarah, a lady whose presence would modify the direction of his reality for eternity.

Michael, a man of knowing taste and scholarly ability, had a voracious interest that frequently driven him on unforeseen excursions. On this specific day, as he wandered through Hyde Park, his faculties were stirred by the hints of chuckling and the scent of sprouting blossoms that drifted through the air. Captivated, he followed the tunes of bliss and jollity, directed by an undetectable hand toward a get-together of close companions.

There, underneath the shelter of an old oak tree, he saw her — a dream that obscured the brilliance of the actual sun. Sarah, with her flowing chestnut twists and eyes the shade of the ocean, radiated an air of both elegance and strength. Her giggling, similar to the tinkling of wind rings, consumed the space and lighted a flash inside Michael's spirit.

Drawn toward her like moth drawn to, Michael drew nearer with a combination of fear and expectation. He ended up captured in her appeal, unfit to oppose the gravitational draw that radiated from her very being. Furthermore, as their eyes met, an association ignited — a gleam of acknowledgment that made no sense and outperformed the limits of simple human perception.

Sarah, as well, felt the attractive energy that popped in the space between them. Her heart enlivened, and a grin graced her lips as she noticed the more odd who had considered wandering into her reality. His eyes, similar to pools of profound consideration, reflected her own yearning for experience and scholarly excitement.

Discussion streamed easily between them, as though they had known one another in another life. They talked about dreams and goals, of the heap of varieties that painted their spirits. Michael, ever the onlooker, was enraptured by the profundity of Sarah's soul, the light that glinted behind her eyes, and the elusive secret that covered her being.

As the sun plunged beneath the skyline, giving occasion to feel qualms about a golden sparkle their environmental factors, Michael marshaled the boldness to request a subsequent gathering. "Would you honor me with your presence for tea, fair Sarah?" he asked, his voice delicate yet touched with a smidgen of weakness.

Sarah, her heart beating inside her chest, delayed the slightest bit, her eyes locked with his. A delicate grin bended her lips as she answered, "I would be really glad, Mr. Craig. I accept there is something else to be investigated in the organization of a close friend."

Subsequently, their excursion of affection and revelation initiated — a journey loaded up with taken looks, murmured admissions, and taken minutes in the midst of the clamoring city. Michael and Sarah delighted in one another's organization, wandering into the profundities of historical centers, going to charming exhibitions at the theater, and participating in energetic conversations that investigated the domains of reasoning and workmanship.

As the weeks transformed into months, their association extended. Michael tracked down comfort in Sarah's delicate touch, her unfaltering help, and the information that he had found a perfect partner who embraced his mannerisms and supplemented his scholarly zest. Sarah, thusly, valued Michael's mind and significant comprehension of her perplexing nature — an affection that outperformed shallow thoughts and flourished in the domain of shared interests and common regard.

It was one ideal night, when the sun painted the sky with tints of rose and gold, that Michael ended up enchanted by Sarah's presence. The couple set out on a comfortable walk around Kensington Nurseries, inseparably, their strides following a way that reflected the excursion of their souls.

Under the shade of a blooming cherry tree, Michael moved in the direction of Sarah, his look relaxed by friendship. "Sarah," he mumbled, his voice conveying the heaviness of an implicit inquiry, "since the day our ways entwined, my heart has been polished off by the flames of affection. Will you do me the distinction of turning into my significant other?"

Sarah's eyes broadened with shock; her breath trapped in her throat. She had known in her heart that this second would show up — a second that would seal their association and tie their coexistences. She connected, her fingers interweaving with his, as she answered with a brilliant grin, "Michael, my affection, my response is an unequivocal yes. You have stirred a fire inside me, a fire that consumes more brilliant as time passes."

In that immortal second, underneath the cherry blooms, Michael and Sarah fixed their affection with a commitment — a guarantee to set out on a deep-rooted experience, connected at the hip, opposing the hardships that lay in their way.

Much to their dismay that this association would push them into a world a long way's past their most out of control imaginings. The secrets that snuck in the profundities of their future would test the strength of their adoration and light a fire of versatility inside their spirits. For fate had an unconventional approach to winding around strings of sentiment, secret, and experience, entwining their lives in an embroidery that challenged traditional ideas of affection and dedication.

As the sun plunged beneath the skyline, creating long shaded areas upon their way, Michael and Sarah started their process as a couple — ignorant about the riddle that looked for them, anxious to disentangle the secrets that lay lethargic inside their common predetermination.

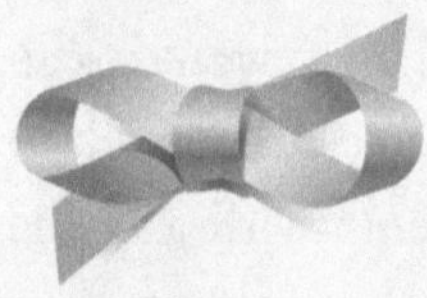

Chapter 3: The Goblin's Trail

The gaslit roads of London oozed a demeanor of interest as Michael Craig wound up submerged in the examination that had consumed his considerations since the disclosure of his significant other's mysterious life as a Troll Slayer. Not entirely set in stone to reveal reality, he dug into the shadowed underside of the city, following the wound way of the trolls and the mysterious wrongdoing association that appeared to control them.

It was on a fog loaded night that Michael wandered into the core of perhaps of London's most famous locale, directed by murmurs and quieted discussions. The roads were shrouded in obscurity, their cobblestones sparkling with the buildup of ongoing precipitation. A feeling of premonition settled inside Michael's chest as he navigated the faintly lit rear entryways, his strides steadfast.

Through the dinky fog, he got a quick look at a bedraggled structure, its exterior disintegrating with disregard. It was supposed to be a center of unlawful exercises — a foundation reputed to be a sanctum for the people who delighted in the profundities of murkiness. Michael prepared himself and circumspectly moved toward the entry, his faculties increased.

As he pushed open the squeaking entryway, he was welcomed by an ensemble of conflicting sounds — a chaos of giggling, the ringing of glasses, and the low mumble of voices, everyone a solicitation to a domain of bad habit and risk. The air was thick with smoke, ringlets of it twirling around the room like ethereal phantoms. Shadows moved on the foul walls, projecting shocking shapes that appeared to murmur mysteries to the people who thought for even a second to tune in.

Michael's eyes shot across the room, concentrating on the essences of the supporters, looking for any smidgen of the trolls' presence. He saw a gathering of men crouched in a corner, their eyes moving subtly, their words shrouded in mystery. Interest lighted inside him, and he drew closer, mixing into the faintly lit openings of the foundation.

Listening in on their discussion, Michael sorted out sections of data — a stealthy organization that worked in the shadows, managing in taken relics, illegal exploitation, and, surprisingly, the control of the actual trolls. The association's impact arrived at a long way past the roads of London, its ringlets broadening like a dangerous plant into each side of society.

His brain burning with the disclosure, Michael withdrew into the evening, his contemplations consumed by the multifaceted snare of misdirection he had uncovered. The subject of Sarah's contribution troubled him like a persevering hurt. Is it true or not that she was mindful of this unavoidable criminal association? Played her part as a Troll Slayer accidentally entrapped her inside their intrigues?

Not entirely set in stone to face reality head-on, Michael got back and looked for comfort in the review — a safe-haven where he had spent endless hours drenched in scholarly pursuit. As he examined volumes of writing, his psyche focused on the association between the trolls and the criminal association. A solitary string arose — a name murmured in quieted tones — a man known as Reginald Blackwood, a famous figure said to be the puppeteer behind the city's evil dealings.

Yet again determined by a newly discovered assurance, Michael wandered into the overly complex roads, his strides directed by an immovable purpose. He searched out sources, those with inside information on Blackwood's activities. The murmurs drove him to the smoke-filled nooks of opium lairs and betting houses, each experience stripping back the layers of the criminal underside.

Through secret discussions and coded trades, Michael figured out how to invade a secret gathering — a get together of people who held the way to disentangling the secrets that laced the trolls and the criminal association. His heart beat inside his chest as he noticed the social event, his eyes dashing from one face to another, looking for any hint of Sarah's presence.

A figure rose up out of the shadows, the embodiment of evil class — Reginald Blackwood himself. Tall and thin, with eyes that appeared to hold the insider facts of the world, he radiated an air of risk and power. The murmurs among the participants avowed his impact, his command over the trolls, and his merciless control of the individuals who served him.

As Michael consumed the sight before him, a glint of acknowledgment glimmered inside his brain. The puzzling photo — the one he had found in the upper room — reemerged in his viewpoints. Might it at some point be conceivable that Blackwood assumed an essential part in Sarah's surreptitious life? Is it safe to say that he was the puppeteer calling the shots, organizing an orchestra of murkiness that compromised all that they held dear?

With the information gathered from the gathering, Michael withdrew into the wellbeing of their home, his psyche turning with plans and systems. He realized that his quest for reality had uncovered a maze of risk, one that expected cautious route. However, he was resolute, filled by the affection for his significant other and the need to safeguard her from the infringing shadows.

Little did Michael had at least some idea that his mission would move him and Sarah further into a hazardous domain — a domain where the lines between sentiment, secret, wrongdoing, and experience obscured, and where their affection and strength would be tried more than ever. As the night sky shrouded London in its hug, Michael set himself up for the fights, not entirely set in stone to reveal the secrets that entrapped his better half and push the criminal association to the brink of collapse.

Chapter 4: The Forbidden Love

The sundown of the night cast long shadows across the concentrate as Michael Craig, consumed by his quest for reality, wound up wrestling with the complexities of his significant other Sarah's covert life as a Troll Slayer. The flashing candlelight washed the room in an ethereal gleam, complementing the heaviness of the disclosures that had agitated their once unspoiled presence.

Sarah entered the review, her face an embroidery of clashing feelings. Her eyes, once loaded up with warmth and delicacy, presently held a flash of misgiving. She moved toward Michael, her strides estimated, as though crossing an imperceptible gorge that had appeared between them.

"Michael," she started, her voice touched with both yearning and anxiety, "the opportunity has arrived for us to stand up to reality that has created its shaded area upon our lives. I comprehend the weight my mysterious life places upon our relationship, yet I beg you to see the affection that ties us, even as our ways wander."

Michael met her look, his demeanor a combination of adoration, disarray, and internal conflict. He got a handle on her hands, his touch looking for comfort and understanding. "Sarah," he murmured, his voice shaking with weakness, "I have long realized that our adoration rises above the limits of show and assumption. However, this new world you occupy, this hazardous way you walk — it challenges my understanding and tests the actual texture of our association."

Sarah's eyes gleamed with unshed tears as she inclined nearer, her voice scarcely a murmur. "Michael, kindly comprehend that I didn't pick this life readily. It picked me, and I embraced it out of obligation to safeguard the guiltless from the detestations that prowl in the haziness. I never expected the cost it would take on our relationship."

Michael's hold fixed on her hands, his heart hurting with clashing feelings. "But," he said, his voice touched with misery, "you kept this piece of yourself stowed away from me, Sarah. How should you generally doubt me enough to share your weights, your battles? Our affection was based on trust, and in covering this mystery, you've broken the establishment whereupon our relationship stands."

Sarah's lips shuddered as she looked for the right words to convey the profundity of her feelings. "Michael, I have dreaded your dismissal, your judgment," she admitted. "I would have rather not troubled you with the obscurity that corrupts my life. Yet, in doing as such, I understand now that I underrated the strength of our adoration. I long for your acknowledgment, your comprehension, even as the heaviness of my mystery takes steps to destroy us."

Michael's eyes mellowed, the tumult inside him giving way to the profundity of his affection for Sarah. He delivered her hands, arriving at up to tenderly stroke her cheek. "Sarah, know this — I love you, profoundly and genuinely," he announced. "Be that as it may, we should go up against the implications of your mysterious life. We can't disregard the dangers it postures to our bliss and security. I'm willing to remain close by, yet we should figure out how to overcome any issues between our universes."

A flash of trust moved inside Sarah's eyes as she inclined toward his touch, her voice a delicate murmur. "Gracious, Michael, your words are an ointment to my injured soul. I can't communicate the help I feel, realizing that our affection gets through even in the midst of the shadows that torment us. Allow us to produce a way ahead, one that permits us to explore the risks that lie ahead, connected at the hip."

They remained in quiet solidarity, the weights of their singular processes merging into a common purpose. Love, savage and enduring, wove its direction through the space between them, bracing their security despite affliction. At that time, they comprehended that their affection was not something delicate, but rather a power that could climate the stormiest whirlwinds.

Days transformed into weeks as Michael and Sarah left on an excursion of compromise, trying to connect the gorge that had developed between them. They participated in discussions that dove profound into the openings of their souls, uncovering weaknesses and fears. Together, they investigated the mind-boggling embroidered artwork of their relationship, understanding that trustworthiness and open correspondence were crucial to recuperate the injuries that had been incurred.

As they explored the intricacies of their affection, Michael likewise looked to grasp the idea of Sarah's mysterious life as a Troll Slayer. He dug into antiquated books and concentrated on the historical backdrop of trolls, looking for bits of knowledge that would permit him to understand the world she occupied. His brain, ever curious, ingested the information like a wipe, step by step disentangling the secrets that had spellbound his better half.

During their common examinations, Michael found that the criminal association weaved with the trolls had long invaded the underside of society, applying impact over those looked for influence and riches. Their activities stretched out a long ways past London, venturing into the haziest corners of the world. Sarah's job as a Troll Slayer, it appeared, was unpredictably connected to her mission to destroy this terrible snare of wrongdoing.

Together, they formulated an arrangement to strike at the core of the criminal association — a daring undertaking that would require cautious coordination and steadfast assurance. Sarah's cozy information on the trolls' functions and Michael's scientific psyche ended up being a considerable mix. They enrolled the assistance of confided in partners — people who had likewise endured because of the association — to shape a considerable power against the infringing haziness.

Days transformed into evenings as Michael and Sarah arranged for their showdown with the criminal association. The moon, a quiet observer to their preliminaries and wins, cast a pale shine upon the city. As they remained at the incline of their main goal, their eyes met, and a quiet comprehension passed between them. This fight would test their adoration as well as their fortitude as they battled to safeguard the blameless and reestablish harmony to a world desolated by obscurity.

The taboo love that had confronted endless preliminaries currently remained as an encouraging sign — a demonstration of the strength of their responsibility and the steadfast force of their bond. As they set out on this risky excursion, they realize that the street ahead would be misleading, loaded up with risk and vulnerability. Be that as it may, together, connected at the hip, they would confront whatever lay in their way, for their adoration opposed shows and rose above the limits of dread.

Thus, with hearts entwined and assurance burning, Michael and Sarah ventured into the conflict, prepared to challenge the shadows that took steps to immerse their lives. Their affection would be their directing light, driving them through the maze of obscurity, and rousing them to recover their common predetermination.

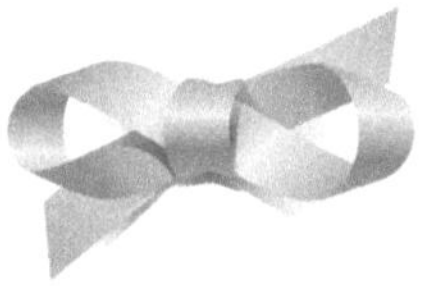

Chapter 5: Partners in Crime

The moon hung high overhead, giving occasion to feel qualms about its shiny gleam the city of London, as Michael Craig and Sarah, his significant other, ready for the fight that lay ahead. They stood together, their hearts adjusted, prepared to face the criminal association that snuck in the shadows, controlling trolls and unleashing ruin upon the honest.

Their arrangement, fastidiously created over long stretches of extreme planning, depended on their extraordinary assets and the help of their confided in partners. Sarah, with her insight into trolls and her ability as a Troll Slayer, would lead the charge against the animals of dimness. Michael, furnished with his insightful psyche and analytical abilities, would reveal the plots of the criminal association and open their chiefs to the illumination of justice.

The last bits of their perplexing riddle made sense as they gathered their group. Among them was Dr. Elizabeth Hastings, a splendid clinical professional whose mastery in toxins and life systems would demonstrate significant in their main goal. Sir Frederick Montgomery, a carefully prepared specialist with a talent for uncovering stowed away bits of insight, loaned his abilities to their goal. What's more, William Patterson, an expert of mask and invasion, would act as their eyes and ears inside the criminal hidden world.

As the clock struck 12 PM, flagging the beginning of their activity, Michael and Sarah traded a look — a quiet seeing passing between them. They realize that the way they had picked would test their actual capacities as well as their determination, their affection, and their common perspective.

Their most memorable objective was a secret distribution center on the edges of London — a cave of unlawful exercises and the reputed base camp of the criminal association. Michael, camouflaged as a dock specialist, invaded the premises, his eyes distinctly noticing the comings and goings of the association's individuals.

In the interim, Sarah wandered into the tangled passages underneath the distribution center, following a path of troll action. Her heart beat in her chest as she slipped into the profundities, her faculties honed by long stretches of preparing. The air developed thick with the odor of wetness and rot; however, she pushed forward, her assurance unflinching.

As she explored the winding entries, she experienced a gathering of trolls, their malignant eyes sparkling in the faint light. With quick and exact developments, she drew her edge, dispatching them individually, her developments a demonstration of her preparation and experience. The conflict of steel against tissue resounded through the passages, an ensemble of risk and assurance.

Back in the stockroom, Michael, tucked away among cases and barrels, revealed proof of the association's illegal exercises. Records, correspondence, and monetary records gave a brief look into the degree of their tasks — a snare of debasement that came to all over, trapping legislators, policing, even the nobility. It was an embroidery of ravenousness and power, woven with the blood of the blameless.

With the data close by, Michael attentively withdrew from the distribution center, rejoining Sarah in the profundities of the passages. Together, they sorted out the riddle of their examination, drawing an obvious conclusion regarding the trolls, the criminal association, and their guileful plans.

Their best course of action took them to a rich house on the edges of London — a get-together spot for the lawbreaker association's chiefs. Camouflaged as visitors going to an elite soiree, Michael and Sarah explored the misleading waters of interest and misdirection, their eyes sharp and their psyches ever watchful.

As they blended with the tip top of society, they noticed the power players who controlled the series of this criminal hidden world. Reginald Blackwood, the cryptic figure supposed to be the puppeteer, moved with a quality of certainty and predominance. His frigid look cleared over the group, surveying his followers and declaring his predominance.

Dr. Elizabeth Hastings, taking on the appearance of a socialite, utilized her appeal and mind to extricate data from clueless visitors. Sir Frederick Montgomery, his sharp faculties sharpened by long stretches of examination, prudently noticed the cooperations, sorting out sections of discussions and signals that alluded to the association's arrangements.

The unease in the room was overwhelming, every heartbeat a sign of the risk that hid underneath the surface. But, in the midst of the tumult, Michael and Sarah tracked down comfort in their mutual perspective. Their eyes met across the room, a quiet trade that said a lot — a sign of the affection and assurance that bound them together.

Their time for activity showed up as the visitors were guided into a rich dance hall, the air thick with expectation. In a venturesome move, Michael uncovered himself, uncovering the crook association's exercises to the clueless group. Disarray emitted as frenzy moved throughout the room, visitors scrambling to get away from the looming breakdown of the criminal domain.

At the same time, Sarah released her abilities as a Troll Slayer, standing up to a crowd of trolls that had been released upon the mayhem. Her edge hit the dance floor with lethal accuracy, the conflict of steel against teeth an ensemble of savage assurance. The fight seethed on, trolls falling individually to her relentless determination.

As the last reverberates of contention died down, Michael and Sarah remained in the midst of the repercussions — a war zone flung with fallen enemies and broke deceptions. Their central goal had succeeded, the criminal association uncovered, and the troll danger killed. However, they realize that the battle against murkiness would be a continuous undertaking.

With their partners close by, they promised to modify, to reestablish request and justice to a city polluted by defilement. Their prohibited love, when a mystery trouble, presently flourished even with difficulty — a demonstration of their steadfast obligation to one another and to the quest for truth.

As they remained in the midst of the remainders of their fight, their eyes locked, and a mutual perspective passed between them. Their organization, fashioned through affection and a typical reason, had demonstrated solid. They realize that their process was nowhere near finished, yet they confronted the future with hearts burning and an assurance that opposed all obstructions.

Together, Michael and Sarah remained as reference points of light in the haziness, their adoration filling in as a directing power as they left on the following section of their experience — prepared to confront the preliminaries that anticipated, connected at the hip, accomplices in both wrongdoings' battling and throughout everyday life.

Chapter 6: Unmasking the Enemy

The aftermath of their triumph over the criminal organization and the goblin threat left London in a state of disarray. Michael Craig and Sarah, his wife, had emerged as formidable forces against the darkness that had plagued the city, but their journey was far from over. They knew that to secure lasting peace, they had to unmask the true puppeteer behind the organization—the elusive Reginald Blackwood.

Days turned into weeks as Michael and Sarah tirelessly delved into the remnants of the organization's operations. They studied the ledgers, scrutinized the correspondence, and pieced together fragments of information, searching for the thread that would lead them to Blackwood's lair.

Their investigation led them down a treacherous path, weaving through the darkest recesses of society. They encountered corrupt officials, shadowy informants, and desperate souls entangled in the web of Blackwood's influence. Each step brought them closer to the truth, but it also exposed them to the danger that lurked around every corner.

One evening, as the moon cast its pale glow upon their study, a breakthrough arrived. Sarah discovered a hidden compartment within one of the ledgers—a compartment that contained a map, meticulously drawn and marked with cryptic symbols. The map held the key to Blackwood's whereabouts—the location of his secret hideaway.

Armed with this newfound knowledge, Michael and Sarah prepared themselves for the final confrontation. They gathered their trusted allies—Dr. Elizabeth Hastings, Sir Frederick Montgomery, and William Patterson—to form a formidable team, united in their purpose. Their plan was bold and audacious—a raid on Blackwood's lair, designed to expose his crimes and bring him to justice.

Under the cover of darkness, they set forth, their steps measured and their minds focused. The night enveloped them, a shroud of anticipation as they followed the map's intricate directions. The path led them through desolate alleyways, abandoned buildings, and hidden passages—a labyrinthine journey that mirrored the complexity of their adversary's mind.

At last, they arrived at their destination—a decrepit mansion nestled on the outskirts of the city. It stood as a testament to the opulence that had been tainted by Blackwood's malevolence. With caution and resolve, they crept through the dilapidated corridors, guided by the flickering light of their lanterns.

As they ventured deeper into the heart of the mansion, a sense of foreboding settled upon them. The air grew heavy with the weight of secrets, and the oppressive silence echoed through the halls. Michael's mind raced, piecing together the puzzle of their investigation, as he anticipated the confrontation that awaited them.

They reached a grand chamber, its walls adorned with faded tapestries and broken statues—a room that seemed frozen in time, a sanctuary for the machinations of a twisted mind. At the center of the room, a figure stood tall, his silhouette framed by the dim light that filtered through the cracked windows.

Reginald Blackwood, the puppeteer of London's criminal underworld, turned to face them. His eyes, cold and calculating, met theirs with an unsettling calmness. There was an air of superiority that emanated from him—a belief that he held the power, the control, over their fate.

"You have come, Mr. Craig and Mrs. Craig," Blackwood said, his voice laced with a hint of amusement. "I must admit, your resilience is admirable. But know this—I am a force that cannot be undone. My influence extends beyond the reaches of your understanding. You are mere pawns in a game that I have already won."

Sarah's grip tightened on her blade, her eyes blazing with determination. "Your reign of darkness ends here, Blackwood," she declared, her voice steady and resolute. "We have uncovered your web of corruption and deceit. Your power is an illusion, built upon the suffering of the innocent. We will expose you and bring justice to those you have wronged."

A sinister smile curved Blackwood's lips, his gaze sweeping over the room. "You underestimate me, Mrs. Craig," he responded, his voice dripping with a perverse delight. "I have seen worlds crumble, empires fall. And yet, here you stand, defiant against the tides of fate. But mark my words—your efforts will be in vain. The darkness cannot be extinguished."

With those chilling words, Blackwood's demeanor shifted. He reached into his coat pocket, producing a vial filled with a swirling, noxious substance. The room seemed to grow colder as he uncorked the vial, the sinister fumes permeating the air. It was a weapon—a potent toxin capable of bringing about an agonizing death.

The battle that followed was fierce and relentless. Michael, Sarah, and their allies fought with unwavering resolve, their skills and determination tested to their limits. Blades clashed, gunshots echoed through the chamber, and the air was thick with the scent of desperation.

Sarah, her movements fluid and precise, engaged in a deadly dance with Blackwood—a battle of wits and physical prowess. She dodged his strikes, her own blade striking with deadly accuracy. But Blackwood, fueled by a deranged determination, fought back with a viciousness born of desperation.

As the battle raged on, Michael noticed a hidden panel within the chamber's walls—a concealed entrance that seemed to hold the promise of escape from the claustrophobic confines of their confrontation. With a swift motion, he signaled to their allies, directing them toward the escape route, their path illuminated by flickering torchlight.

Meanwhile, Sarah and Blackwood continued their deadly duel, the clash of steel reverberating through the room. She fought not only for her own survival but for the innocents whose lives had been irrevocably altered by Blackwood's wicked machinations. Her heart pounded within her chest as she sought to expose the true depths of his depravity.

In a moment of daring, Sarah deftly disarmed Blackwood, her blade poised at his throat. The room fell silent, the weight of their confrontation hanging heavy in the air. The man who had held London in the grip of fear now stood at the precipice of his own demise.

"You have lost, Blackwood," Sarah declared, her voice a resolute echo. "Your reign of darkness ends here."

A flicker of defeat crossed Blackwood's face, his gaze a mix of fury and resignation. "You may have won

this battle," he hissed, his voice laced with bitterness, "but the darkness within men's souls will endure. It cannot be vanquished."

With those haunting words, Blackwood slumped to the ground, defeated but defiant until the very end. The room grew still, the tension dissolving into a sense of profound relief. Michael approached Sarah, his eyes filled with admiration and love, as they surveyed the aftermath of their confrontation.

The battle against Blackwood had come to an end, but their journey was not yet complete. They understood that the darkness within the human heart could never be fully eradicated. But armed with their love, their resilience, and the knowledge that they had the power to make a difference, they stood ready to face whatever trials awaited them.

As they made their way out of the dilapidated mansion, their steps marked by the echoes of their triumph, Michael and Sarah knew that their partnership—forged through love, trust, and a shared purpose—had been instrumental in unmasking the enemy that had threatened the city they loved. Together, they would continue their fight for justice, guided by the unwavering light of truth.

Little did they know that their journey had only just begun—that new mysteries, challenges, and adventures awaited them beyond the threshold of Blackwood's lair. But with their bond unbreakable, their determination unyielding, and their love a steadfast beacon, they faced the future with hearts aflame, ready to unveil the mysteries that awaited them on the horizon.

Chapter 7: Tangled Alliances

The reverberations of their triumph against Reginald Blackwood and his criminal domain resounded through the roads of London. Michael Craig and Sarah, his significant other, rose up out of the shadows as legends who had battled against the haziness and won. However, they realize that their work was nowhere near finished, for new difficulties looked for them in the unpredictable woven artwork of their common predetermination.

In the fallout of their victory, the couple ended up at a junction — a snapshot of break in the midst of the turmoil that had consumed their lives. They withdrew to the recognizable comfort of their review, looking for shelter in the glow of their adoration and the thought of their subsequent stages.

As they sat peacefully, the delicate sparkle of the gas lights projecting an encouraging air around them, a thump at the entryway intruded on their viewpoints. Michael rose from his seat, interest provoked, and made the way for uncover a figure shrouded in murkiness — a man with puncturing eyes that appeared to hold a universe of mysteries.

The man presented himself as Edmund Sinclair, a puzzling person with binds to the criminal hidden world, looking for reclamation for his past sins. He made sense of that he had been an individual from Blackwood's association, pressured into their positions through coercion and control. In any case, seeing the profundity of their barbarities had lighted a longing inside him to set things straight and help those battling against the obscurity.

Fascinated by Sinclair's proposition, Michael welcomed him into the review, where Sarah noticed their visitor with a combination of wariness and interest. They listened eagerly as Sinclair uncovered secret information — data that could reveal insight into the many-sided snare of collusions that had supported Blackwood's realm.

Sinclair discussed a shadowy figure — a strong and puzzling individual referred to just as The Rook — who had called the shots in the background, controlling both Blackwood and the criminal association. This disclosure creeped them out, for it implied that their triumph over Blackwood had only been a little piece of a lot bigger game.

Driven by their voracious hunger for justice, Michael and Sarah saw an open door in Sinclair's information. They perceived the benefit of including an insider inside the criminal hidden world — a person who could assist with exploring the deceptive waters that lay ahead. With mindful positive thinking, they chose to shape a coalition with Sinclair, understanding that trust should be acquired, yet it was feasible to trust that recovery.

Days transformed into weeks as they unwound the mind-boggling strings that bound The Rook to Blackwood's criminal association. They wandered into the profundities of London's underside, looking for replies from witnesses, finding leads, and sorting out pieces of data like criminal investigators gathering a complicated riddle.

Their examination drove them to a secret organization of people who had experienced under The Rook's vindictive impact. Every one conveyed scar, both physical and profound, caused by the baffling figure who snuck in the shadows. These people, when pawns in The Rook's down, presently looked for reclamation and justice, conforming to Michael and Sarah's objective.

Among their newly discovered partners was Rebecca Hawthorne, a savage and wise lady whose information on The Rook's tasks demonstrated priceless. She had gotten through her own frightening encounters because of the crook engineer and looked to keep others from facing a similar outcome.

Together, Michael, Sarah, Sinclair, Rebecca, and their developing coalition fashioned a way through the obscurity. Theirs was a sensitive dance — a dance of trust, faithfulness, and mutual perspective. Each step in the right direction carried them nearer to exposing The Rook and destroying the curved realm he had fastidiously constructed.

Be that as it may, The Rook, similar to a ghost, stayed slippery — a manikin ace calling the shots from the shadows. His compass reached out a long ways past London, with ringlets that stretched out into the most elevated echelons of force. To expose him, Michael and Sarah would need to infiltrate the inward sanctums of society, where privileged insights were watched with savage assurance.

Their examination drove them to an extravagant ball, a social occasion of the city's first class — an occasion where The Rook's impact was supposed to be especially articulated. Masked in their best clothing, Michael and Sarah explored the mind-boggling dance of social behavior, their eyes distinctly noticing the cooperations and motions that held the hints to their quarry's character.

As they blended with the gentry, a feeling of disquiet settled inside them. The murmurs that continued afterward conveyed stories of interest, defilement, and secret partnerships. Obviously to expose The Rook, they would need to unwind the trap of misdirection that reached out a long way past the criminal hidden world — a web that snared both companion and enemy.

As they continued looking for replies, Michael and Sarah experienced recognizable countenances — people they had once thought about partners, yet who currently appeared to be covered in vagueness. Loyalties were tried, unions addressed, as they battled to isolate companion from enemy in this multifaceted dance of double dealing.

It was during an essential second, as the symphony played a frightful tune and the dance hall whirled with polish and interest, that Sarah saw an inconspicuous trade between two people — a look that held a mysterious language. Following her senses, she motioned toward Michael, and together, they watchfully followed the baffling pair as they got away into the confounded passageways of the chateau.

Their interest drove them to a secret chamber — a safe-haven where illegal mysteries were murmured and coalitions were fixed in blood. Inside the room, they found an assortment of concealed figures, their personalities taken cover behind lavish camouflages. It was an undercover social event — a gathering coordinated by The Rook himself.

Heart beating inside his chest, Michael perceived the unobtrusive strategic maneuvers, the hidden discussions that alluded to The Rook's aims. Eagerly, he saw as The Rook ventured forward, his personality actually hid underneath a veil, his voice a vile his that creeped them out.

"Welcome, regarded visitors," The Rook broadcasted, his voice bound with a frigid moxy. "This evening, we accumulate to additional our advantages, to fix the strings that hold society in our grip. Our power stretches out a long way past the scope of the law, for we work in the shadows, where the principles are our own to control."

Michael's psyche dashed, sorting out the sections of data he had accumulated, drawing an obvious conclusion that had evaded him as of not long ago. The genuine degree of The Rook's impact turned out to be agonizingly clear — his snare of trickery extended all over, entrapping the individuals who trusted themselves to be blameless.

As The Rook proceeded with his discourse, Michael and Sarah traded a knowing look. They comprehended that exposing this baffling figure would require immovable assurance, shrewd, and the partnerships they had developed. The tangled web that bound them all would require cautious moving — a fragile dance on the slope of risk.

With newly discovered resolve, they withdrew from the secret chamber, their brains on fire with systems and plans. They realize that their best course of action would decide their own destiny as well as the destiny of the individuals who had endured at The Rook's hands. The collusion they had manufactured, loaded with intricacies and insider facts, would be put to a definitive test as they arranged to disclose the genuine substance of their enemy.

Thus, Michael, Sarah, Sinclair, Rebecca, and their partnership of reclaimed spirits wandered further into the core of murkiness, their strides directed by the quest for justice and the unfaltering light of truth. They realize that the way they track was slippery, yet outfitted with their determination and the tangled partnerships they had shaped, they were prepared to confront whatever lay ahead, to expose The Rook and push his rule of fear to the brink of collapse.

Chapter 8: Pursuit and Escape

London's cloudy roads, covered in haze and secret, set up for the constant quest for The Rook. Michael Craig and Sarah, his significant other, alongside their partners — Sinclair, Rebecca, and their recently manufactured collusion — left on a hazardous mental contest, following the confounding figure through the overly complex city.

Their interest drove them through the most obscure corners of London — a path set apart by stowed away sections, secret gatherings, and the murmured gossipy tidbits about The Rook's impact. As they followed the scraps left by their enemy, they turned out to be very much in the know about the peril that hid every step of the way.

The pursuit strengthened one night as they cornered a low-positioning individual from The Rook's association. Cross examination yielded a fragment of data — a potential place where The Rook had withdrawn to refocus and design his best course of action. It was a feeble distribution center on the edges of the city — an unnoticeable design that filled in as a lair of mysteries.

Under the front of dimness, Michael, Sarah, and their partners met upon the stockroom, their means quick and their faculties uplifted. The air was weighty with expectation as they crawled through the shadows, their developments as quiet as the murmur of a phantom.

After entering the stockroom, they ended up in the midst of a hive of crime — a trap of people participated in illegal arrangements, their countenances concealed by veils of obscurity. The scene reflected the contorted dance of force that The Rook had arranged — a many-sided embroidered artwork woven with trickiness and debasement.

As Michael and his sidekicks pushed forward, they experienced obstruction — a gathering of vigorously equipped gatekeepers, faithful to The Rook and able to safeguard their lord at any expense. Fight followed, the conflict of steel and the resonating roar of discharges swirling all around. Sarah's cutting edge, shining in the faint light, struck valid and quick, her abilities as a Troll Slayer demonstrating important.

Their joined strength and assurance won, overwhelming the watchmen and making a way more profound into the stockroom. They explored through secret chambers and winding passages, their eyes checking each corner for indications of their quarry. A lot was on the line — the quest for The Rook held the commitment of justice as well as the possibility to disentangle the perplexing trap of debasement that had entrapped London.

It was inside the profundities of the stockroom that they at last cornered The Rook — a subtle figure disguised underneath a veil, his actual character at this point unclear. His voice, trickling with malice, slice through the air, insulting them with subtle provocations and commitments of tumult.

"You might have followed my path, yet you can't appreciate the profundities of my power," The Rook jeered, his words bound with egotism. "London is mine to control, its mysteries mine to take advantage of. You are nevertheless bugs, humming needlessly against the walls of my domain."

Michael met The Rook's look, his eyes igniting with an undaunted assurance. "Your rule of murkiness closes here," he pronounced, his voice consistent and unfaltering. "We will divulge your actual face and uncover the snare of duplicity you have turned. Justice will win."

A strained quietness fell upon the room as Michael and his partners ready to confront The Rook in a skirmish of brains and wills. The air snapped with expectation, the heaviness of their interest arriving at its apex. They comprehended that their activities would have sweeping outcomes — a gradually expanding influence that would reshape the city's fate.

However, similarly as they prepared themselves for the last a conflict, a progression of blasts shook the distribution center, shaking the actual underpinnings of their interest. Smoke surged through the air, clouding their vision and projecting a cloak of turmoil upon the scene.

In the midst of the disarray, The Rook quickly jumping all over the chance to make his departure — a shadowy consider vanishing along with the murkiness, leaving just murmurs of malignance afterward. Michael and his partners battled against the confusing climate, frantically endeavoring to follow The Rook's escaping strides.

Their interest drove them through a labyrinth of trash and flares, the popping heat perplexing their purpose. They ran with enthusiasm, assurance scratched upon their faces, declining to allow their quarry to fall through their grip. In any case, The Rook, similar to a ghost, appeared to liquefy into the shadows, leaving just transitory hints of his presence.

As they arose out of the stockroom, their breaths weighty and their bodies fatigued, they looked at the city, presently land with the gleam of their interest. Yet again the Rook had evaded them, getting past them like a ghost. Yet, they realize that their pursuit had not been in that frame of mind for they had acquired significant bits of knowledge into his tasks, his organization, and the profundity of his corruption.

With a combination of disappointment and assurance, Michael went to his mates. "We might not have caught The Rook this evening," he said, his voice touched with a fearless assurance, "however we have revealed the degree of his debasement. We should pull together, accumulate our solidarity, and proceed with the pursuit. London's future relies upon it."

His words reverberated with his partners; their eyes loaded up with a common perspective. They had confronted difficulties and hesitant adversaries, yet their assurance consumed more splendid than at any other time. Their quest for justice wouldn't be dissuaded by The Rook's slippery strategies — it would fuel their determination and reinforce their securities.

Thus, as the air got and the coals free from their interest gleamed in the evening, Michael, Sarah, Sinclair, Rebecca, and their collusion arranged to come to life. They realized that the way forward would be deceptive, the impediments unrealistic, however outfitted with their steadfast assurance and a common perspective, they were prepared to pursue the shadows, to seek after The Rook until justice prevailed.

Chapter 9: The Goblin King's Lair

The quest for justice drove Michael Craig, Sarah, and their partners further into the complicated embroidered artwork of London's criminal hidden world. With each step, they revealed new layers of defilement, misleading, and the evil maneuvers that had tormented the city. However, in the midst of the quest for The Rook, another danger lingered — an old abhorrent that mixed in the shadows: the Troll Lord.

Bits of gossip about troll action had arrived at Michael and Sarah's ears — a resurgence of these vindictive animals that unleashed destruction and planted dread among the honest. The Troll Lord, a figure of dimness and disorder, remained at the focal point of their pernicious tasks, calling the shots from his secret sanctuary.

Driven by their enduring obligation to safeguard the city and its kin, Michael and Sarah wandered into the failed to remember profundities where the trolls had made their home. Equipped with their insight into troll killing and directed by their common perspective, they set out to face the Troll Lord and stop his rule of fear.

The way to the Troll Lord's sanctuary was deceptive — a maze of moist passages and ghostly caves, enlightened exclusively by the faint light of their lamps. The air developed weighty with the odor of sogginess and rot, an unpropitious indication of the malignant presence that looked for them.

As they dug further into the underground maze, the hints of abandoning and murmured reverberations encompassed them. The trolls, detecting their presence, ready for the fight to come. Michael and Sarah prepared themselves, their hearts burning sincerely, as they prepared their weapons and ready to deal with the animals directly.

The conflict of steel against hook resonated through the passages — an orchestra of risk and resolve. Sarah's edge hit the dance floor with lethal accuracy, each strike a demonstration of her long stretches of preparing as a Troll Slayer. Michael, his scientific brain ever working, tracked down their enemies' shortcomings, taking advantage of them with determined strikes.

As they pushed forward, the force of their fight expanded. The trolls battled with a savage craze, their numbers apparently interminable. However, Michael and Sarah battled on, determined by the chances stacked against them. They realize that the stakes were higher than any time in recent memory — that the Troll Lord's loss would carry rest to the city, scattering the apprehension that had grasped its occupants.

At long last, after what felt like an unfathomable length of time of furious battle, they arose into a tremendous chamber — the core of the Troll Ruler's den. The air was thick with malice, and the faint light uncovered a sight that creeped them out.

Roosted upon an improvised privileged position, encompassed by his troll cronies, sat the Troll Lord — a twisted figure with red hot eyes and spiked teeth. His presence oozed a substantial air of murkiness and power. He scoffed at Michael and Sarah, savoring the valuable chance to vanquish the individuals who thought for even a second to challenge his territory.

"You have wandered into my space, silly humans," the Troll Ruler murmured, his voice a throaty snarl. "However, know this — the force of trolls is timeless. We are the sign of bedlam and dread, and no human can remain against us."

Michael and Sarah met the Troll Lord's look with steadfast determination. "Your rule of fear closes here," Sarah proclaimed, her voice ringing with power. "We are not simple humans — you misjudge the strength of our assurance and the force of justice. Plan to confront your retribution."

With those words, the fight initiated — a conflict of wills and sharp edges that reverberated through the chamber. Michael and Sarah battled with a steadiness brought into the world of their mutual perspective, their developments composed and their hearts burning with a craving to safeguard the honest.

The Troll Ruler, energized by his noxious power, released his cronies upon them. The trolls went after with a savage furor, their hooks and teeth trying to destroy their enemies. However, Michael and Sarah, their bond strong, held their ground, avoiding the assault with ability and accuracy.

As the fight seethed on, Sarah figured out how to arrive at the Troll Lord's privileged position, her edge ready to strike the conclusive blow. In any case, the Troll Lord, detecting the impending danger, released a staggering rush of dim energy — a power that sent Sarah plunging in reverse, her body running into the sinkhole wall.

Michael's heart loaded up with pain as he saw Sarah's fall. With a restored assurance, he battled through the crowd of trolls, his means energized by affection and distress. He arrived at Sarah's side, supporting her in his arms, his voice loaded up with pain and assurance.

"Sarah, my adoration, hang on," he murmured, his voice gagged with feeling. "Together, we will conquer this dimness. You are the light that guides me."

Sarah's eyes shuddered open, her look meeting Michael's with a furious assurance. "Try not to flounder, my affection," she murmured. "Rout the Troll Ruler. Stop this rule of dread."

With those words, Michael rose from Sarah's side, his determination braced by her solidarity. He confronted the Troll Lord by and by, their eyes secured in a clash of wills. The chamber popped with energy as they conflicted — a demonstration of the conflict of light and dimness, trust and dread.

In a last, unequivocal strike, Michael's edge tracked down its imprint — a blow that pierced the core of the Troll Ruler. The chamber fell quiet, the trolls frozen in dismay as their chief disintegrated to the ground. The obscurity that had held the city for such a long time was at last scattered.

With the loss of the Troll Lord, Michael and Sarah arose successful — a guide of light in the midst of the shadows. They realize that their fight against obscurity could never genuinely be finished, yet their victory in the Troll Ruler's den was a demonstration of their faithful determination and the force of affection.

As they rose up out of the underground maze, their means directed by the gleam of the sun, they conveyed with them the information that their activities found carried harmony and security to the city. The trolls, dissipated and crushed, represented no further danger.

Michael and Sarah, their hearts limited by their common perspective and unflinching affection, remained as watchmen of London — a city perpetually changed by their faithful devotion to justice. The reverberations of their triumph resonated through the roads, a demonstration of the unstoppable soul of the individuals who thought for even a second to challenge the dimness.

What's more, as they viewed the city they had safeguarded, their eyes met — a quiet seeing passing between them. Their excursion, however loaded with risk and vulnerability, had manufactured a bond that rose above the common. Together, they would confront anything preliminaries looked for them, their adoration sparkling like an encouraging sign in the midst of the shadows, everlastingly laced in their quest for justice.

Chapter 10: Desperate Measures

The triumph over the Troll Lord had carried a brief break to London, yet Michael Craig and Sarah, his better half, realize that their work was nowhere near total. The ringlets of defilement actually waited, and another danger lingered not too far off — a foe who tried to take advantage of the void left by The Rook and the Troll Lord's defeat.

As they refocused with their partners, Sinclair, Rebecca, and the reclaimed spirits who had joined their goal, a need to get moving held the air. The city was defenseless, its kin needing insurance. The ideal opportunity for frantic measures had come, for they needed to go up against this new foe before their plans grabbed hold.

In the faintly lit study, the gathering accumulated around a table jumbled with guides, records, and obscure notes. Michael's scientific brain was working diligently, sorting out the pieces of data they had assembled up to this point. Each lead, each hint would be essential in exposing this new adversary.

Sinclair, his eyes loaded up with a newly discovered assurance, made some noise. "I have learned of a social event — a mystery meeting of persuasive figures who try to fill the power vacuum left by The Rook and the Troll Lord. They plot to reshape the city as per their own curved cravings."

Rebecca gestured, her look savage. "These people stand firm on footings of force and impact. They take cover behind decent exteriors, their actual aims concealed by their status. We should uncover them and foil their arrangements before it's past the point of no return."

Michael, his brain humming with procedures, realize that they required a conclusive move — a determined hit that would profoundly impact their foes. "We should invade this social affair, assemble proof of their plans, and divulge reality to individuals of London," he said, his voice unfaltering. "We should show them the profundities of this debasement and rally their help against the people who try to take advantage of their trust."

The arrangement came to fruition — a trying activity that necessary accuracy, mystery, and an eagerness to take a chance with everything. Michael, Sarah, Sinclair, Rebecca, and their partners would expect new personalities, masking themselves as visitors welcome to this undercover social affair. They would mix with the tip top, notice their activities, and accumulate proof that would uncover their real essence.

Under the front of haziness, they advanced toward the great house where the social occasion was to occur. Their hearts hustled with expectation as they moved toward the overwhelming entryways — a passage to a universe of mysteries and double dealing.

Inside, the lavish assembly hall was buzzing with the chat of compelling figures. The air was weighty with interest as Michael and his partners, their countenances taken cover behind veils, explored the sensitive dance of blending and perception. They tried to disentangle the strings of trick, to observe the genuine goals of the people who grasped the city's destiny.

As they traveled through the group, their ears tuned to scraps of discussions and murmured reports, they got looks at the dim underside that spoiled this apparently refined society. Bargains were broadcasted in quieted vibes, partnerships shaped and broken, all in quest for power and impact.

Michael, his sharp faculties sharpened by long periods of analyst work, saw a specific bunch of people — a close assembling in an isolated corner. There, in the midst of the glimmer of gem and flashing candlelight, a vile plot unfurled.

Sinclair, who had charmed himself among these people, murmured the subtleties to Michael and Sarah. They learned of the plans that looked to control the city's economy, exploit the powerless, and fix the hold of defilement. It was a snare of misdirection and insatiability, woven by the people who wore veils of decency.

As time passes, their need to get moving uplifted. They realized they needed to act quickly, for the more extended these people stayed in power, the further their ringlets of defilement would sink. The ideal opportunity for frantic measures had come.

In a determined move, Michael moved toward the social occasion, his disposition created and his voice bound with power. "Lovely people," he declared, his words slicing through the prattle of the room, "I should draw out into the open the real essence of this get-together — a social occasion of trickery and treachery. The city of London is in danger, and you are the modelers of its destruction."

A quieted quietness slipped upon the room; everyone's eyes fixed on Michael's figure. He proceeded, his voice consistent and steady. "Your plans, your plots, have been uncovered. Your actual goals uncovered. Individuals of this city merit better — a future liberated from your debasement and double-dealing."

The assembled figures, at first dazed by Michael's disclosure, immediately recuperated. Outrage and dread moved quickly over their countenances, supplanted by an aggregate assurance to safeguard their not well gotten gains. They respected Michael and his partners with hatred, understanding that their painstakingly built veneer had disintegrated.

A man, apparently the head of this stealthy social event, ventured forward. His voice trickled with presumption as he tended to Michael. "You want to remain against us? You misjudge our power and impact. London is our own to control."

In any case, Michael stood firm, his eyes loaded up with unflinching purpose. "Your power lays on the enduring of the honest," he proclaimed, his voice reverberating with power. "In any case, we stand joined against your oppression. We will uncover your violations and carry justice to those you have violated."

With those words, disorder emitted in the assembly hall. Watches moved to catch Michael and his partners, their unwaveringness purchased with commitments of riches and impact. Be that as it may, Michael, Sarah, Sinclair, and Rebecca retaliated, their assurance unfaltering. The room turned into a milestone — a tornado of steel, clench hands, and frantic battles.

In the midst of the tumult, Michael's scientific brain stayed at work longer than required, looking for a getaway highway, a method for getting their endurance. He motioned toward Sarah and their partners, and with a quick movement, they ran towards a hid exit — their main any desire for evading catch.

They went through faintly lit passageways, their strides reverberating through the unwanted corridors. Monitors sought after them steadily, their yells and reviles shutting in. In any case, Michael and his partners pushed forward, driven by the information that their main goal was not even close to finish.

With a last explosion of solidarity, they arose onto the clamoring roads of London, their breaths weighty and their bodies wounded. They had endured the frantic measures they had taken, yet their fight against debasement was not even close to finished. Their characters currently known to the individuals who tried to safeguard their not well gotten gains, they would need to take on new pretenses, new methodologies, to proceed with the battle.

Michael went to his partners, a flash of assurance in his eyes. "However, we face vulnerability and risk," he said, his voice loaded up with conviction, "we won't be discouraged. We will refocus, revamp our powers, and uncover these bad people so that the world might see. Frantic measures will turn into our weapon, our method for endurance in this fight for justice."

As they vanished into the evening, their personalities shrouded in shadows, Michael, Sarah, Sinclair, and Rebecca realize that their quest for justice would require forfeits and dangers. They had seen the genuine profundities of defilement, and their purpose consumed more brilliant than any time in recent memory.

London's fate remained in a precarious situation — a city on the verge, got between the powers of murkiness and the people who battled to safeguard its spirit. Notwithstanding difficulty, they stood joined together, their frantic measures a demonstration of their unfaltering obligation to the quest for truth and the victory of justice.

Chapter 11: Betrayal and Redemption

The room was shrouded in a climate of disquiet as Michael Craig and his partners, Sarah, Sinclair, and Rebecca, accumulated in their mystery safehouse. The glimmering candlelight cast moving shadows upon the walls, reflecting the vulnerability that hung weighty in the air. A feeling of disloyalty had wormed its direction into their middle, taking steps to disentangle the delicate bonds they had fashioned as they continued looking for justice.

Michael, ever the adroit analyst, couldn't disregard the signs. Sinclair, when a man looking for reclamation, had become progressively removed, his face tormented by shadows. The doubts had become too conspicuous to even think about overlooking, and Michael realize that the time had come to stand up to the fermenting storm head-on.

With a grave air, Michael required a gathering. The room developed quieted as the four partners assembled around a well-used wooden table, their eyes fixed on Sinclair, anticipating his clarification.

"Sinclair," Michael started, his voice estimated and firm, "we have noticed an adjustment of your disposition — a moving of loyalties, maybe. It is of most extreme significance that we address this matter before it compromises our main goal. Talk your reality, for our partnership depends on trust."

Sinclair's eyes dashed anxiously around the room, his hands squirming with disquiet. The heaviness of their look pushed ahead upon him, and he realize that the ideal opportunity for obscurity had reached a conclusion. Taking a full breath, he met Michael's unflinching look.

"I should admit," Sinclair started, his voice loaded up with a combination of culpability and lament, "that I hold information that could change the direction of our battle against Master Aldridge's defilement. Be that as it may, this information comes at an individual expense and raises questions about my dedication."

Michael inclined forward, his eyes puncturing and unfaltering. "You talk about private expense and questions," he answered. "We are very much aware of the penances expected in this fight. Be that as it may, presently, like never before, we should stand together. Share what you know, Sinclair, and let reality guide us."

Sinclair's voice shuddered somewhat as he proceeded, his look moving between his buddies. "I was once profoundly inserted inside Ruler Aldridge's organization," he admitted, his voice weighted with the heaviness of his past sins. "The mysteries I hold, the obscurity I have seen, jeopardize every one of us. Yet, assuming we are to uncover Ruler Aldridge's real essence, we should stand up to a much more prominent hazard — a risk that could shake the actual underpinnings of our coalition."

The room fell into a weighty quiet, the gravity of Sinclair's words soaking in. The partners confronted a significant decision — to confide in Sinclair's expectations or to throw him away, gambling with the openness of their own weaknesses.

Sarah, her eyes loaded up with a blend of concern and assurance, ended the quiet. "Sinclair," she started, her voice quiet yet touched with alert, "in the event that what you say is valid, we should listen to you. Yet, grasp this — we track a tricky way, one that requests immovable dependability. Double-cross us, and the outcomes will be serious."

Sinclair gestured, appreciation and assurance scratched upon his face. He paused for a minute to consistent himself before he spread out his arrangement — an arrangement that would lead them profound into the core of Master Aldridge's fortification, where the puppetmaster's actual power lay hidden.

Their main goal was clear — to uncover Ruler Aldridge's snare of defilement and deal with him. The way forward was hazardous; however, the stakes were too high to even think about turning around now. Michael, Sarah, Sinclair, and Rebecca comprehended that recovery and selling out moved intently together, and just through solidarity and trust might they at some point explore the slippery street that lay ahead.

Thus, with unflinching hearts and brains, they put their focus on the premonition post that housed the puppetmaster's privileged insights. Reclamation and selling out remained in a precarious situation, entwining their destinies in a dance ancient. Reality looked for them, shrouded in dimness, as they arranged to wander into the core of the tempest.

Chapter 12: The Final Showdown

The room was steeped in an atmosphere of anticipation and tension as Michael Craig, Sarah, Sinclair, and Rebecca prepared for the ultimate confrontation—the final showdown with Lord Aldridge. The den of shadows, with its flickering candlelight and lingering air of deceit, served as the battleground for their last stand against the puppetmaster of London's corruption.

As the four allies stood shoulder to shoulder, their resolve unwavering, a hush fell over the chamber. The time for words had passed, replaced by the weight of imminent action. The truth, like a dormant beast, pulsated beneath the surface, ready to be unleashed upon the world.

Michael's eyes met Sarah's, their unspoken understanding conveying a shared determination. He then turned his gaze to Sinclair, who had come so far on his journey of redemption, and Rebecca, the voice of reason and strategy. Together, they were an unstoppable force—a united front against the darkness that had engulfed the city.

With a resolute nod, Michael took the lead, stepping forward to face Lord Aldridge, who sat upon his throne of deception. The puppetmaster wore a sly smile, his eyes glinting with a twisted satisfaction.

"So, Craig," Lord Aldridge sneered, his voice dripping with malicious amusement, "you have come to challenge me in my own domain. How bold of you, but know that you are but a pawn in this game of power."

Michael's voice rang out, firm and unwavering, cutting through the tension in the room. "No longer, Aldridge," he declared, his gaze steady. "Your reign of corruption ends here. We have uncovered your web of deceit, and the truth will be revealed to all."

Lord Aldridge let out a cold, mirthless laugh. "The truth, Craig? Do you truly believe that the truth has the power to change the world?" he scoffed. "The world is built upon lies and manipulations. Power is the only currency that matters."

Sinclair stepped forward; his voice filled with conviction. "Aldridge, I have seen the depths of your corruption. I have lived it," he stated, his words ringing with the weight of his own redemption. "But there is always a choice—a chance to rise above the darkness. We will bring your machinations to light, and justice will prevail."

Lord Aldridge's eyes flickered with a mix of anger and defiance. "Justice, Sinclair? Redemption?" he spat; his voice filled with venom. "Those are but fleeting notions, illusions that crumble in the face of true power. You will find no salvation here."

Sarah, her voice calm yet brimming with determination, stepped forward. "Lord Aldridge, your power rests upon the suffering and misery of others," she asserted, her eyes blazing with righteous fury. "We stand united against you, not just for ourselves, but for all those who have been victimized by your cruelty."

Rebecca, the embodiment of intellect and strategy, surveyed the chamber, her mind working at lightning speed. "Aldridge," she interjected, her voice laced with a quiet intensity, "we have uncovered your secrets, your network of corruption. The evidence is damning, and the world will know the truth. Your grip on power is slipping."

Lord Aldridge's face contorted with a mix of rage and desperation. He rose from his throne, his voice filled with a newfound ferocity. "You think you can expose me? You think you can defeat me?" he roared, his words reverberating through the chamber. "You are nothing compared to the might I possess."

With those words, Lord Aldridge signaled his guards, and they advanced upon Michael and his allies. The room erupted into chaos as the clash of steel filled the air. The allies fought with a fierce determination, their movements precise and coordinated, their minds attuned to the rhythm of battle.

Michael, drawing upon his years of experience, analyzed the guards' patterns, seeking weaknesses to exploit. With each strike, he incapacitated his adversaries, never losing sight of his ultimate goal—to expose the truth and bring Aldridge to justice.

Sarah, her agility unmatched, moved with grace and precision. She deflected blows with ease, her keen instincts guiding her actions. Her weapon danced through the air, striking true against her opponents, while protecting her allies with unwavering vigilance.

Sinclair fought with a newfound purpose, channeling his past mistakes into a force for redemption. The weight of his guilt pushed him forward, his blade striking with precision and fury. His years of darkness now served as a catalyst, fueling his resolve to dismantle Aldridge's empire of corruption.

Rebecca, with her sharp intellect, analyzed the battlefield, strategizing their movements and exploiting openings in their adversaries' defenses. She directed her allies, orchestrating their actions like a maestro conducting an intricate symphony of justice.

As the battle waged on, the room trembled with the echoes of clashing steel and resolute determination. Michael and his allies fought with unwavering resolve, inching closer to their ultimate objective—to expose the truth and dismantle Lord Aldridge's web of corruption.

In the midst of the chaos, Michael's gaze met Sarah's, and their unspoken understanding propelled them forward. With a swift and coordinated assault, they broke through the guard's defenses, clearing a path toward Lord Aldridge.

Their footsteps echoed through the chamber as they approached the puppetmaster, their eyes filled with the fire of justice. Lord Aldridge, his face contorted with fury and fear, realized that his reign was crumbling, that his web of deceit was unraveling before his very eyes.

"You cannot defeat me!" Lord Aldridge spat, his voice a venomous hiss. "I am the master of this city, and you are nothing more than insects in my grand design."

Michael's voice cut through the tumultuous air, steady and resolute. "Your grand design ends here, Aldridge," he declared, his eyes locking onto the puppetmaster's. "The truth will prevail, and your empire of corruption will crumble. Your power is an illusion, built upon the suffering of others."

With a final surge of determination, Michael, Sarah, Sinclair, and Rebecca closed in on Lord Aldridge. In a swift and decisive move, they disarmed him, stripping away his facade of power.

Lord Aldridge, his eyes filled with rage and defeat, sank to his knees. The weight of his crimes and the revelation of his true nature crushed him. In that moment, the puppetmaster of London's corruption was dethroned, brought to his knees by the relentless pursuit of justice.

The room fell into a heavy silence as Michael and his allies stood over the fallen Lord Aldridge. The truth had triumphed, and justice had been served. The city would no longer be held captive by the puppetmaster's grip.

In the next chapter, London will reckon with the aftermath of Lord Aldridge's downfall. The allies will face the consequences of their actions and navigate a city forever changed by the exposure of its darkest secrets. The journey for redemption and justice may be far from over, but with their unwavering resolve, they will continue to fight for the light that shines beyond the shadows.

Chapter 13: Healing Wounds

The echoes of battle still lingered in the chamber as Michael Craig, Sarah, Sinclair, and Rebecca stood over the fallen Lord Aldridge—the puppetmaster of London's corruption. The room, once shrouded in darkness and deceit, now basked in the dim glow of victory. But with victory came the realization that the battle had left wounds, both physical and emotional, that needed tending.

As the silence settled, broken only by the soft flickering of candlelight, Michael turned his attention to his allies. Their faces bore the marks of the fierce struggle they had endured—bruises, scratches, and weariness etched upon their features. It was time to heal the wounds, both seen and unseen, that the fight had inflicted.

"Sarah," Michael said, his voice filled with concern, "attend to our fallen comrades and ensure they receive the care they need. Sinclair, help me tend to the wounded guards. We must show mercy even to those who fought against us."

Sarah nodded, her gaze filled with a mix of weariness and determination. She knelt beside the fallen guards, offering comforting words and assessing their injuries. The horrors of battle had stripped away the illusion of enemies and allies, reminding her of the shared humanity that bound them all.

Sinclair joined Michael as they approached the wounded guards, their weapons now discarded, replaced by a different kind of resolve. They administered aid, binding wounds and offering words of solace. It was a small act of redemption—a reminder that even those who had been caught in the web of corruption could find their way back to the light.

Rebecca, with her keen intellect and unwavering determination, began to assess the damage inflicted upon Lord Aldridge's fortress. She cataloged the evidence of his crimes, collecting the fragments that would serve as testament to the truth they had unearthed. The city would need to reckon with its past, to confront the darkness that had permeated its very core.

As the allies tended to the wounded and collected evidence, a realization washed over them—the battle had been won, but the war against corruption was far from over. The exposure of Lord Aldridge was only the beginning, a catalyst for change that would require a collective effort to rebuild and heal the scars that had marred the city.

Days turned into weeks, and the wounds, both physical and emotional, began to heal. London, forever changed by the revelations of its darkest secrets, grappled with the aftermath of Lord Aldridge's downfall. The city's inhabitants, once living in the shadow of corruption, now sought solace and hope in the newfound light of truth.

Michael, his detective instincts ever sharp, took it upon himself to ensure that justice prevailed. He worked tirelessly, meticulously piecing together the evidence against Lord Aldridge and his network of corruption. The pursuit of justice was not just a personal endeavor—it was a duty owed to the countless victims who had suffered under the puppetmaster's reign.

Sarah, her spirit undeterred, became a beacon of strength and compassion. She worked tirelessly to provide support to those affected by the revelations, lending a listening ear and a comforting presence. The wounds of the city ran deep, but Sarah's unwavering determination to heal and rebuild brought a sense of hope to those who had been betrayed.

Sinclair, forever changed by his journey of redemption, sought to make amends for his past transgressions. He used his knowledge of Lord Aldridge's network to assist in dismantling the remnants of corruption that still lingered. Each step he took towards redemption was a testament to the power of choice and the capacity for change.

Rebecca, the strategic mind behind their success, navigated the complexities of rebuilding and reform. She worked tirelessly to forge alliances with those who shared their vision of a just and transparent London. The wounds of the city were not just physical—they ran deep within its institutions, and it would take a collective effort to restore trust and create lasting change.

In the wake of Lord Aldridge's downfall, a new chapter began for London—a chapter of healing, rebuilding, and redemption. The scars of corruption would not fade overnight, but the allies remained steadfast in their commitment to justice. The battle against the darkness had left its mark, but the resilience of the human spirit would prevail.

And so, London embarked on a journey of transformation, guided by the tireless efforts of Michael, Sarah, Sinclair, and Rebecca. They had faced the depths of darkness and emerged stronger, united in their pursuit of a city free from corruption.

The wounds of the past would heal, and the light of truth would guide them towards a brighter future.

In the next chapter, as the city rebuilds, a new threat emerges, testing the resolve of Michael and his allies. They will face a choice—to retreat into the shadows or to rise once more, ready to confront the challenges that lie ahead. The journey for justice and redemption continues, weaving its way through the intricate tapestry of London's streets.

Chapter 14: Unraveling Secrets

Following Master Aldridge's destruction, London wound up on the cliff of change. The city, when entrapped in a snare of defilement, presently relaxed in the gleams of truth and justice. Notwithstanding, as the scars of the past started to recuperate, another danger arose, creating a shaded area over the partners and their hard-battled triumph.

Michael Craig, ever the cautious criminal investigator, detected that the fight against debasement was nowhere near finished. A disquiet settled inside him, a murmur of risk hiding underneath the surface. He realized that it was his obligation, close by Sarah, Sinclair, and Rebecca, to go up against the new danger head-on.

As the partners reconvened in their mystery safehouse, the glimmering candlelight moved upon their countenances, reflecting the vulnerabilities that waited to them. Michael, his sharp eyes looking over the room, ended the quiet.

"We have vanquished one foe, yet it appears to be that the obscurity actually waits," he started, his voice bound with a blend of assurance and concern. "There are privileged insights yet to be uncovered, and we should unwind them assuming that we are to guarantee the enduring opportunity of our cherished city."

Sarah, her eyes gleaming with a fire of assurance, shouted out. "We should stay careful," she asked, her voice loaded up with resolve. "Debasement rots in the shadows, and we should be ready to defy it, regardless of how profoundly it is covered up."

Sinclair, his way to reclamation entwined with their common mission, gestured in arrangement. "We have seen the profundities of London's haziness," he recognized, his voice touched with a combination of regret and recharged reason. "Be that as it may, our process isn't yet finished. There are more insider facts to uncover, more fights to battle."

Rebecca, her psyche a maze of technique and examination, interposed. "We should be careful," she cautioned, her voice consistent. "Our previous triumph has uncovered us, made us defenseless. There are the individuals who might try to douse the light we have lighted. We should expect their moves and remain one stride ahead."

With their motivation revived, the partners set out on another examination — a maze of signs and secret insights that anticipated disclosure. They wandered into the profundities of London, where murmurs of unfairness and duplicity waited in each back street and each shadowy corner.

Their quest for justice drove them through a labyrinth of interconnected strings, every one uncovering another layer of defilement. From the most elevated echelons of capacity to the haziest underside of society, they followed the ringlets of, not entirely settled to uncover reality that lay stowed away.

As they dug further into their examination, Michael's sharp psyche started to come to an obvious conclusion. An example arose — a snare of interwoven interests and secret plans that came to a long ways past Master Aldridge's rule. The debasement they had battled against was profoundly imbued, its foundations snared in the actual texture of the city.

Sarah, ever the compassionate soul, looked for comfort and data from the underestimated voices of the city — the failed to remember survivors of debasement. She paid attention to their accounts, their murmured admissions, assembling the sections of truth that had been hushed for a really long time. Their voices turned into a signal, directing her towards the core of the murkiness they tried to vanquish.

Sinclair, troubled by his past and energized by his freshly discovered reclamation, assumed the risky undertaking of penetrating the covert organizations that flourished in the city's underside. He gambled with openness, drawing upon his past associations with explore the misleading waters of trickery. Through his endeavors, he uncovered the secret figures that called the shots, controlling the predetermination of London.

Rebecca, equipped with acumen and instinct, dissected the proof they uncovered, sorting out the riddle with accuracy. She recognized the central participants — the strong figures whose impact rose above borders and obscured the lines among good and bad. With every disclosure, the shadows withdrew, and the way towards justice became clearer.

Their examination disclosed a frightening truth — a tremendous organization of defilement, stretching out a long ways past Master Aldridge's grip. The web they had thought disentangled ended up being complicatedly woven, its strands venturing into the most noteworthy echelons of force. They had uncovered a mysterious society — a secrecy of powerful figures who plotted to keep up with their extremely tight grip on the city.

In the following part, Michael and his partners will face the mysterious society head-on, gambling with everything in their quest for justice. As they explore the deceptive territory of force and interest, they will confront selling out, unforeseen collusions, and a fight that will test their determination as far as possible. The mysteries that have putrefied in the shadows of London will be uncovered, and the destiny of the city will remain in a critical state.

Chapter 15: The Missing Puzzle Piece

The room developed faint as the night sun plunged underneath the skyline, creating long shaded areas that moved upon the walls. Michael Craig, Sarah, Sinclair, and Rebecca assembled around a well-used wooden table, their countenances scratched with a combination of assurance and exhaustion. The examination concerning London's mysterious society had driven them down a misleading way, yet an unaccounted-for puzzle part actually escaped them — a disclosure that would open the genuine degree of the intrigue.

Michael, his foreheads wrinkled in profound idea, filtered through the records and signs that lay dissipated across the table. His brain dashed, interfacing the sections of data like an expert riddle solver looking for the last unaccounted-for part. The mystery society's unpredictable snare of defilement had uncovered numerous bits of insight, however one significant inquiry stayed unanswered.

"We've gained huge headway," Michael started, his voice consistent yet touched with dissatisfaction. "In any case, there is a missing connection — a piece of the riddle that would uncover the brains behind everything. We really want to track down that unaccounted for part assuming we are to destroy this snare of debasement for the last time."

Sarah, her look fixed on the gleaming light at the focal point of the table, thought about their situation. "There should be a secret association we haven't revealed," she pondered, her voice touched with a blend of assurance and interest. "Somebody in the background, calling the shots and organizing this fantastic connivance."

Sinclair inclined forward, his eyes igniting with a restored feeling of direction. "We've experienced many strong figures, yet there should be one at the middle — a puppetmaster controlling the predeterminations of others," he added, his voice resounding with conviction. "We really want to dig further, follow the paths that have been let alone."

Rebecca, her fingers following the shapes of a guide that spread across the table, contributed with a sharp insight. "We should backtrack our means, look at the associations we've proactively revealed," she recommended, her voice loaded up with the assurance of a planner. "The unaccounted-for part is there, flying under the radar. We simply have to check out at the proof according to an alternate point of view."

With restored center, the partners followed their examination, returning to the proof and associations they had previously settled. They poured over reports, reconnaissance film, and witness declarations, looking for that slippery connection that would unwind the last string of the connivance.

Days transformed into evenings as they dove further into their investigation, their assurance unwavering. The city's privileged insights murmured to them, their voices becoming stronger with every disclosure. Gradually, an example arose — a name that resounded through the passages of force.

It was a name that had surfaced in their examination previously — a figure of impact and riches, known to be a cryptic influence representative. Ruler Reginald Worthington — a name that deserved admiration and struck dread into the hearts of the people who thought for even a moment to cross him.

Michael's eyes augmented as the pieces made sense. "Worthington," he mumbled, the name conveying weight and importance. "He's been available every step of the way — the consistent idea interfacing the powerful figures we've experienced."

Sarah, her psyche dashing, reviewed the experiences with Worthington — a man who had consistently stayed slippery, his actual intentions concealed underneath layers of appeal and interest. "He's the unaccounted-for puzzle part," she pronounced, her voice loaded up with a blend of fervor and worry. "Worthington is the genius behind the connivance, the one organizing this fantastic plan."

Sinclair, his look solidifying with resolve, gestured in understanding. "We should defy Worthington, uncover his real essence to the world," he declared, his voice resounding with the assurance of a tracked down man reclamation. "He has held London hostage for a really long time."

Rebecca, her psyche working at lightning speed, concocted a game plan. "We should accumulate unquestionable proof — evidence that will push Worthington to the brink of collapse," she recommended, her voice bound with vital accuracy. "When we have the proof, we can uncover him and destroy the mysterious society for the last time."

With their way presently clear, the partners set out on their last mission — to assemble the proof that would uncover Master Reginald Worthington's real essence. They realized the dangers were high, that all their moves would be watched by the eyes of the strong world class. Yet, their purpose stayed relentless — they wouldn't rest until justice won.

In the following part, the partners will confront their most noteworthy test yet — the showdown with Ruler Reginald Worthington. They will explore a slippery trap of force and duplicity, gambling with all that to deal with the puppetmaster. The mysteries that have putrefied in the shadows of London will be uncovered, and the destiny of the city will remain in a precarious situation. The last fight for justice and reclamation is standing by.

Chapter 16: Chasing Shadows

The moon hung high in the night sky, projecting a silver shine over the roads of London as Michael Craig, Sarah, Sinclair, and Rebecca left on their central goal to stand up to Master Reginald Worthington — the slippery puppetmaster behind the mysterious society. Their strides reverberated through the abandoned rear entryways; the heaviness of their motivation substantial in the air.

They moved with a determined accuracy; their faculties uplifted as they explored the dim underside of the city. The murmurs of peril appeared to move on the edge of their cognizance, a steady indication of the shadows that snuck everywhere.

Michael, his analyst senses sharpened by long stretches of involvement, drove the way, his eyes checking the environmental elements for any indications of risk. He realized that they were navigating a precarious situation, wavering among openness and achievement. The chase after Worthington resembled pursuing shadows, each lead getting past them, abandoning just hints of his impact.

Sarah, her means light yet deliberate, moved quietly next to Michael. Her heart hustled with a blend of expectation and fear, her look dashing from one shadow to another. She realized that the showdown with Worthington would test their guts, their capacity to penetrate through the cloak of trickiness that had covered London for a really long time.

Sinclair, his past interweaved with the city's haziest privileged insights, paused his breathing as he followed intently behind. The heaviness of his recovery moved him forward, his determination resolute. He had once strolled in the shadows, yet presently he tried to vanquish them, to carry light to the spots where obscurity had flourished.

Rebecca, her psyche working like clockwork, ingested everything about their environmental factors. She examined the trap of associations that had driven them to this second, her instinct directing their way. The pursuit for Worthington was a skirmish of brains, a mental contest where a lot was on the line and the results critical.

Their interest welcomed them to a neglected stockroom on the edges of the city — a spot that stunk of failed to remember insider facts and undercover dealings. The once clamoring center of action currently stood ruined; its walls stained with the reverberations of the past.

As they ventured into the faintly lit stockroom, the air thick with expectation, they realize that the last a showdown looked for them. The reverberations of their strides resonated through the unfilled space, an eerie sign of the fights they had battled and the penances made en route.

A glimmering light caused them to notice a figure remaining at the furthest finish of the distribution center — an outline shrouded in murkiness. It was Ruler Reginald Worthington, the puppetmaster who had arranged London's debasement from the shadows.

With a blend of assurance and watchfulness, Michael ventured forward, his voice slicing through the quietness. "Worthington," he started, his voice consistent and faithful, "your rule of duplicity closes here. The opportunity has arrived for you to confront the results of your activities."

Worthington's eyes, loaded up with a blend of self-importance and noxiousness, met Michael's look. "Ok, Craig," he jeered, his voice trickling with loftiness, "you have ended up being a remarkable persistent issue for me. Yet, do you really accept that you can challenge the way and impact that I have?"

Sarah, her voice fearless, joined Michael's side. "We have seen the profundities of your debasement, Worthington," she expressed, her words injected with conviction. "Your power is based upon the enduring of others. Yet, the opportunity has arrived for justice to win."

Sinclair, his sword primed and ready, ventured forward. "We have confronted the shadows you cast upon this city," he proclaimed, his voice reverberating with the reverberations of his own recovery. "Furthermore, we won't waver in that frame of mind of justice. Your rule closes now."

Rebecca, her eyes glimmering earnestly, surveyed the circumstance with a sharp insight. She realized that the showdown would be hard, that Worthington wouldn't give up easily. Yet, she stayed unfaltering in their common mission — to cut down the puppetmaster and reestablish uprightness to the city they cherished.

The strain in the distribution center arrived at its top as the partners went head-to-head against Worthington. It was a skirmish of wills, a conflict of belief systems that would decide the destiny of London. The air snapped with an electric energy, accused of the heaviness of their aggregate reason.

In the following section, the last fight for justice and reclamation will unfurl — a fight that will test the restrictions of their determination and power them to face their own weaknesses. As the shadows join and mysteries disentangle, the partners will find that the genuine power lies not in the dimness, but rather in the unfaltering quest for truth.

Chapter 17: Love Tested

The distribution center was covered in a scary quietness as Michael Craig, Sarah, Sinclair, and Rebecca went head-to-head against Ruler Reginald Worthington, the puppetmaster who had controlled London's destiny from the shadows. The air snapped with strain, every heartbeat a demonstration of the heaviness of their motivation.

As their eyes met, Worthington's lips twisted into a vindictive grin. "Ok, the legends of justice," he jeered, his voice dribbling with toxin. "You figure your equitable goal can conquer the power that I use? You misjudge me."

Michael, his voice consistent regardless of the weightiness of the circumstance, answered, "Worthington, your power is based on the enduring of blameless lives. We won't allow you to keep on controlling this city. The ideal opportunity for justice has come."

Sarah, her eyes igniting earnestly, ventured forward. "We have seen the profundities of your debasement, the lives you have obliterated," she announced, her voice firm. "Love and sympathy will beat your wound feeling of force."

Sinclair, his hold fixing on his weapon, added, "We have confronted dimness previously, and we have arisen more grounded. Your rule closes now, Worthington. It is the ideal opportunity for the illumination of truth to uncover your foul play."

Rebecca, her psyche dashing with systems, broke down their rival with a sharp mind. She knew that overcoming Worthington would require something beyond actual strength — it would require steady purpose and the force of affection to beat the obscurity that consumed him.

Yet, as the showdown unfurled, another test arose — one that tried their actual strength as well as their close to home grit. Worthington's look fell upon Sarah, a brutal flicker in his eyes. "Ok, Sarah," he said, his voice bound with a blend of malevolence and something likened to want. "How love can cloud one's judgment. Do you genuinely accept that you can remain against me, knowing reality with regards to your darling Michael?"

Sarah's heart skirted a thump as she took a gander at Worthington, her eyes loaded up with a combination of outrage and skepticism. "What do you mean?" she requested, her voice shaking. "What have you done?"

Worthington's grin augmented, savoring his disclosure. "Your dearest Michael, the regarded investigator, has confidential — a mysterious that will break the groundwork of your adoration," he insulted, relishing the trouble carved across Sarah's face.

Michael's eyes restricted, a gleam of concern blending in earnestly. "Worthington, your endeavors to plant friction will fizzle," he expressed, his voice unflinching. "Sarah and I are limited by an affection that is more grounded than any trickery you could summon."

Sinclair, his dependability to Michael unflinching, ventured forward, his voice loaded up with conviction. "Worthington, we know your strategies — attempting to split apart us. However, love will win, and we will stand joined against your unfairness."

Rebecca, ever the voice of reason, noticed the circumstance with a sharp eye. "Worthington, your endeavors to control feelings won't divert us from our main goal," she contributed, her voice quiet and undaunted. "Love is a power that can vanquish even the most obscure of insider facts. We won't be influenced."

As the showdown increased, Sarah's heart throbbed with vulnerability. She saw Michael, looking for reality behind Worthington's insults. She had consistently confided in him certainly; however, question presently worried the edges of her psyche.

Michael, his voice loaded up with crude trustworthiness, intertwined Sarah's hand with his. "Sarah, there are things I have not uncovered," he conceded, his eyes locked with hers. "Yet, our adoration is based on trust. Believe that I will uncover reality eventually, yet for the present, we should zero in on the fight before us."

Sarah's heart faltered briefly, however as she investigated Michael's eyes, she saw the earnestness and love that had consistently characterized their relationship. With a gesture, she reaffirmed her confidence in him, understanding that their adoration would be tried however not broken.

The partners, their purpose supported by adoration and trust, confronted Worthington with unfaltering assurance. They battled against his duplicities, his endeavors to plant disagreement, and together they demonstrated that affection could endure the most obscure of difficulties.

In the following part, as the fight seethes on, the partners will reveal the last bits of insight that falsehood concealed in the shadows. They will uncover Worthington's actual expectations, destroy the mysterious society, and carry justice to London. Love will be tried, yet it will likewise be the main impetus that drives them forward, helping them to remember the force of solidarity and immovable dedication.

Chapter 18: Redemption and Sacrifice

The last fight against Master Reginald Worthington and the mysterious society seethed on, the air thick with strain and the fragrance of distress. Michael Craig, Sarah, Sinclair, and Rebecca battled with resolute determination, their developments liquid and deliberate. They had made significant progress to be influenced by dread or uncertainty. Reclamation and penance interweaved as they stood up to the profundities of obscurity that had tormented London for a really long time.

Sinclair, troubled by his past and driven by his mission for reclamation, battled with a furious assurance. Each swing of his weapon conveyed the heaviness of his excursion, the longing to make up for his transgressions. He realized that reclamation lay not as would be natural for him but rather in his activities, and during the most intense part of the conflict, he tried to safeguard his partners and purge his own spirit.

Sarah, her heart hurting with the heaviness of Worthington's disclosures, battled with a reestablished feeling of direction. Love and trust turned into her safeguard and sword, enabling her to confront the difficulties that took steps to destroy them. With each strike, she fought Michael Craig t for justice as well as to safeguard the adoration she imparted to

Michael, realizing that their bond was more grounded than any trickery.

Rebecca, her mind sharpened by the excursion of unwinding privileged insights, planned each move with accuracy. She saw the penances that lay ahead, the dangers they would need to take to guarantee triumph. Her brain worked indefatigably, computing the best game-plan while keeping the security of her confidants at the very front. She comprehended that their battle was for the city as well as for the opportunity of reclamation — for them and those impacted by the mystery society's debasement.

Michael, the sturdy criminal investigator, drove the accuse of a consistent hand and a psyche honed by long stretches of examination. His obligation to justice was unfaltering, yet presently it was interlaced with the affection he imparted to Sarah. The disclosures that had surfaced taken steps to subvert their bond, yet he realize that the way to recovery required penance. He battled for the city as well as to demonstrate that adoration could win over the shadows that tried to destroy them.

As the fight seethed on, the partners confronted imposing enemies — individuals from the mysterious society who gripped to the power and honor that Worthington had guaranteed them. The conflict of steel against steel swirled around, the reverberations resounding through the neglected distribution center. The fight tried their solidarity, their assurance, and their eagerness to make penances for everyone's benefit.

Amidst the turmoil, Worthington's voice slice through the turbulent air. "You want to overcome me?" he sneered; his voice bound with egotism. "I'm the puppetmaster, arranging the destiny of this city. You are only simple pawns in my great plan."

Michael, his eyes locked onto Worthington's, stood tall and steadfast. "Your plan closes here," he pronounced, his voice conveying the heaviness of truth. "London will be liberated from your oppression, and justice will win."

The fight arrived at its peak as the partners pushed forward, their assurance unfaltering. However, with each step they took, a penance became unavoidable. Sinclair, filled by his quest for recovery, stepped before a deadly blow implied for Sarah, his activities a demonstration of the extraordinary force of penance.

The acknowledgment of Sinclair's penance washed over the partners, their hearts weighty with a combination of sadness and appreciation. His demonstration of benevolence filled in as an update that reclamation frequently required penance, and that the battle for justice conveyed a lofty expense.

In the outcome of Sinclair's penance, the tide of the fight turned. With reestablished resolve, the partners pushed forward, their developments filled by the memory of their fallen companion. The mysterious society individuals fell individually, their hold on power disintegrating underneath the heaviness of justice and love.

At last, Michael and Sarah defied Master Reginald Worthington, their eyes blasting earnestly. Together, they released their last attack, their affection and solidarity filling in as a safeguard against Worthington's frantic endeavors to stick to control. In a last venture of reclamation and penance, they pushed him to the brink of collapse.

As the residue settled, a weighty quietness occupied the room. The partners remained in the midst of the destruction, their bodies battered and their spirits tried. They had accomplished triumph, yet it had come at an incredible cost.

In the following section, the partners will wrestle with the consequence of their fight, grieving the deficiency of their confidant and retribution with the scars that the battle has abandoned. In any case, they will likewise find comfort in the information that their penances were not to no end — that reclamation, love, and justice can win over even the haziest of mysteries.

Chapter 19: Final Reckoning

The outcome of the fight left the partners remaining in the midst of the vestiges of the unwanted distribution center, their bodies tired and their hearts weighty with the heaviness of penance. The reverberations of their victory blended with the waiting distress for their fallen friend, Sinclair. They realize that their process was approaching its end, yet the last retribution looked for them.

As Michael Craig, Sarah, and Rebecca reviewed the destruction, their eyes met, quietly recognizing the cost that their quest for equity had taken. They had battled against the defilement that had tormented London, unwound mysteries, and persevered through selling out. Presently, it was the ideal opportunity for the last retribution — the perfection of their excursion.

Rebecca's sharp insight started to sort out the leftover parts of the mystery society's organization. "We should guarantee that all remainders of the intrigue are exposed," she declared, her voice firm. "Really at that time could London at any point genuinely mend."

Michael, his analyst impulses still sharp, gestured in arrangement. "We want to uncover each association, each person who has propagated this trap of debasement," he expressed, his voice conveying the heaviness of his assurance. "They should confront equity for their wrongdoings."

Sarah, her heart weighty with distress for Sinclair's penance, added, "We owe it to Sinclair to guarantee that his penance was not to no end. His memory will direct us as we stand up to the last remainders of the mysterious society."

With their determination reestablished, the partners set out on their last examination — a mind boggling dance of revealing secret collusions and finding the people who had sidestepped their interest hitherto. Each hint drove them more profound into the underside of the city, to the core of the haziness that had tormented London for a really long time.

As they uncovered each secret association, their interest carried them eye to eye with persuasive figures — people who had used power from the shadows, taking advantage of the weaknesses of the city's foundations. The partners, equipped with proof and steady assurance, faced them with reality they had long tried to cover.

Individually, the mysteries were uncovered, and the strong figures disintegrated under the heaviness of their responsibility. The last retribution showed up, as the partners remained under the steady gaze of the courtrooms, introducing their proof, and it was guaranteed that equity. London saw the destruction of the individuals who had once held it hostage.

In any case, as the city started its excursion of recuperating, the partners, as well, wrestled with their own scars. The injuries caused upon their spirits during the fight remained, waiting tokens of the penances made chasing after equity. They grieved Sinclair's nonattendance, his memory perpetually carved in their souls.

In the peaceful minutes that followed, Michael, Sarah, and Rebecca tracked down comfort in each other's presence. Love, tried and tempered by the difficulties they had confronted, turned into their anchor — a wellspring of solidarity that directed them through the murkiness and towards the light.

Together, they considered the excursion that had carried them to this point — the fights battled, the privileged insights unwound, and the penances made. They had explored the slippery waters of defilement and arisen on the opposite side, everlastingly changed however loaded up with trust for a more promising time to come.

Chapter 20: Resolution and New Beginnings

London remained at the slope of another period as Michael Craig, Sarah, and Rebecca embraced the goal that had come after their long and difficult fight against debasement. The mysteries that had rotted in the shadows were currently uncovered, and the city started its excursion of recuperating. In the fallout of their victory, the partners tracked down comfort in realizing that justice had won, and they were prepared to embrace fresh starts.

As the sun rose over the city, providing reason to feel ambiguous about its brilliant light the roads, Michael, Sarah, and Rebecca accumulated at their mystery safehouse — a spot that had turned into a safe-haven all through their central goal. The room, once loaded up with pressure and assurance, presently radiated a feeling of quiet and help.

Michael, his look mirroring the heaviness of their excursion, tended to his friends. "We have progressed significantly," he started, his voice loaded up with a blend of appreciation and reflection. "Through the hardships, we have battled for justice and disentangled the insider facts that had held our cherished city hostage."

Sarah, her eyes sparkling with a hint of something better over the horizon, gestured in understanding. "We have

97

confronted double-crossing, tried our adoration, and saw penances," she recognized, her voice delicate yet fearless. "However, we arose more grounded, joined in our quest for truth and the longing to carry light to the most obscure corners."

Rebecca, her astuteness presently unwound from the snare of intrigue, offered her understanding. "Our work here is nowhere near finished," she expressed, her voice conveying a note of assurance. "However, with the mysterious society destroyed, the groundworks of defilement have disintegrated. It is the ideal opportunity for fresh starts — for ourselves and for the city."

With a common perspective, the partners set out on their singular, still up in the air to add to the modifying of London. Michael, ever the analyst, got back to his insightful work, focused on guaranteeing that justice kept on winning. His name became inseparable from the victory over defilement, and his standing as a boss of truth spread all through the city.

Sarah, directed by her humane heart, zeroed in her endeavors on recuperating the injuries caused upon the minimized and powerless. She turned into a voice for the voiceless, committing herself to social causes and loaning her solidarity to those out of luck. Her thoughtful gestures carried desire to the wrecked and roused others to stick to this same pattern.

Rebecca, with her essential psyche and sharp keenness, directed her concentration toward reconstructing the foundations that had been debilitated by debasement. She worked indefatigably to change strategies, guaranteeing that straightforwardness and responsibility turned into the support points whereupon the city's future would stand. Her endeavors revived the administration of London, imparting a reestablished feeling of trust among its residents.

As time elapsed, the scars left by the fight started to blur, supplanted by a feeling of good faith and reestablishment. The city flourished under the full concentration's eyes of Michael, Sarah, and Rebecca. Together, they framed an impressive collusion — supporting each other, partaking in their triumphs, and loaning some assistance when required.

However, it was in their own lives that the partners tracked down their most prominent bliss. Michael and Sarah's adoration developed further as time passes, their bond produced in the cauldron of misfortune. They wedded, their association an image of versatility and the victory of affection over obscurity. Their common obligation to justice kept on driving their undertakings, yet it was their relentless love for each other that gave them comfort and pleasure.

Rebecca, as well, tracked down comfort in her own life. She set out on an excursion of self-revelation, understanding that her essential psyche and humane heart could track down satisfaction past the battle against debasement. She shaped profound associations with similar people, fashioning new companionships and embracing the conceivable outcomes that life brought to the table.

Furthermore, as London recuperated, another section started — one of trust, solidarity, and an aggregate obligation to a superior future. The scars of debasement became tokens of the city's flexibility, while the victory over murkiness filled in as a demonstration of the unstoppable soul of its occupants.

In the last goal and fresh starts, the partners tracked down satisfaction in their singular ways while staying joined in their common perspective. The tradition of their fight against debasement would persevere, filling in as an update that even despite murkiness, justice, love, and solidarity could win.

Thus, as the city pushed ahead, the names of Michael Craig, Sarah, and Rebecca became inseparable from boldness, truth, and unflinching commitment. They had confronted the best difficulties, disentangled the most profound mysteries, and arose as encouraging signs in a city that had been moved by obscurity. Together, they had achieved a fresh start — a section in London's set of experiences characterized by reclamation, goal, and the commitment of a more promising time to come.

Chapter 21: Shadows of the past

The roads of London relaxed in the shine of the morning sun, warmth reinvigorating the city had endured the hardship of debasement. Michael Craig, Sarah, and Rebecca wound up amidst a fresh start — a part of mending and restoration. The consequence of their fight against the mysterious society had carried equity to London, however the shadows of the past actually waited, an indication of the penances made and the injuries that required repairing.

As the threesome strolled along the cobbled roads, the city hummed with action, its occupants approaching their day-to-day routines. Michael, his sharp investigator impulses never dulled, noticed the indications of progress — changes coming to fruition, establishments revamped on a groundwork of straightforwardness, and a thriving feeling of trust. In any case, underneath the surface, he detected that not all injuries had mended, and there were remainders of the mysterious society that kept on hiding in the shadows.

Rebecca, with her essential brain, brought up the areas that actually required consideration — the weak networks needing support, the waiting ringlets of debasement that had not been altogether annihilated, and the well-established doubt among the general population. She knew that while the fight had been won, the battle for London's spirit was not altogether finished.

Sarah, her merciful heart directing her activities, contacted those impacted by the general public's defilement — offering comfort to the families destroyed, giving guide to those out of luck, and attempting to reconstruct a feeling of local area that had been cracked by dimness. She realized that the injuries of the city would carve out opportunity to recuperate, similarly as her own heart would get some margin to repair after the disclosures about Michael.

As they strolled, Michael's considerations floated to his significant other, Sarah. Their affection had endured the hardship, yet the insider facts he had kept still weighed intensely on his heart. He realized that he expected to uncover reality — a reality that would additionally test their bond. He longed for a new beginning, liberated from the shadows that had tormented them, yet he realize that the past couldn't be quickly deleted.

One night, as the sun plunged underneath the skyline, creating long shaded areas over the city, Michael and Sarah wound up in the isolation of their safehouse — a spot that held the two recollections of win and distress. With crushing sadness, Michael started to talk, uncovering the bits of insight he had held back.

"Sarah," he said, his voice touched with weakness, "there is something I want to confess to you — a mysterious that I have kept stowed away." He took a full breath, preparing himself for her response. "During our examination, I had encountered the mysterious society before we even met. I was at that point mindful of their impact in the city."

Sarah's eyes enlarged with shock; however, she stayed quiet, permitting Michael to proceed.

"I joined the examination to cut them down, to safeguard the city and its kin," Michael made sense of, his look locked with hers. "However, when I found that you were a troll slayer, I expected that my past would corrupt your view of me. I feared losing you, so I kept my insight stowed away."

Sarah tuned in, her heart conflicted between understanding and hurt. "Michael," she said delicately, "I wish you had confided in me enough to share this weight. Our affection is based on trust, and we might have confronted this together."

Michael gestured; his regret apparent. "You're correct, Sarah. I ought to have confided in you, and please accept my apologies for the aggravation my quietness caused you," he conceded, going after her hand. "Yet, realize that my obligation to equity and our affection has forever been relentless. I needed to safeguard you, to protect you from the haziness that encompassed us."

Sarah investigated Michael's eyes, her heart relaxing. "I know that now," she answered, her voice loaded up with empathy. "Furthermore, I comprehend the reason why you did what you did. We've confronted such a great deal together, and we've arisen more grounded. We can confront the shadows of the past together as well."

With that, Michael and Sarah found comfort in one another's hug, their affection beating the shadows that had tormented them. The heaviness of their common encounters brought them closer, restricting their hearts considerably tighter than previously.

In the interim, Rebecca proceeded with her endeavors to carry enduring change to the city. She worked enthusiastically, organizing with authorities and local area pioneers to address the waiting remainders of debasement and offer help to those generally impacted. Her mind and empathy demonstrated important as she explored the intricacies of reconstructing a city that had been damaged by haziness.

In any case, the city's reestablishment didn't come without difficulties. As the partners dug further into the shadows, they found that a few individuals from the mysterious society had figured out how to dodge catch, mixing into the texture of London like ghosts. Their subtle presence perplexed Michael, advising him that the fight was not yet completely won.

With each piece of proof uncovered, another layer of interest arose, driving the partners on a deceptive way. The shadows of the past appeared to become more obscure, and they understood that the mysterious society had left an enduring inheritance — one that would require steadfast devotion to destroy completely.

Even with these difficulties, the partners drew strength from their solidarity and assurance. They realize that the battle for London's spirit was nowhere near finished, yet they additionally perceived the flexibility of their city and the force of affection to beat even the haziest of shadows.

As they proceeded with their quest for equity and mending, they realize that the tradition of their fight would persevere — a getting through demonstration of the victory of good over evil, love over treachery, and solidarity over obscurity. London's fresh start had been hard-battled, and the city presently remained on the cliff of a more promising time to come, everlastingly molded by the mental fortitude and commitment of Michael Craig, Sarah, and Rebecca — the unstoppable triplet who had confronted the shadows of the past and arose triumphant.

Chapter 22 : Elusive Trail

The undeniable trends moved throughout London as the city kept on reconstructing after the dull long periods of defilement. Michael Craig, Sarah, and Rebecca, not set in stone to uncover the last remainders of the mysterious society that kept on sidestepping catch. The subtle path had driven them to a maze of double dealing, and with each turn, the shadows of the past appeared to extend.

One morning, as the haze settled over the city, Michael ended up immersed in his analytical work. The excess individuals from the mysterious society were like apparitions, falling through his grip with each lead he sought after. His diligence, notwithstanding, was immovable, and he realize that an advancement could be not far off.

Sarah, ever the guide of empathy, had drenched herself in her work with the weak networks. She had turned into a mainstay of help for those impacted by the general public's debasement, giving solace and help to the people who required it most. Notwithstanding the difficulties she looked in her own life, her obligation to equity and her kinsmen stayed unshaken.

Rebecca's essential brain worked indefatigably, drawing an obvious conclusion that would lead them to the leftover individuals from the mysterious society. Her investigation of the proof carried them nearer to reality; however, the maze appeared to move and change, making their interest all the seriously difficult.

One night, as the sun set over the city, projecting a brilliant shade over the roads, the partners accumulated in their safehouse. Disappointment and exhaustion waited in the air, an unmistakable difference to the expectation that had energized their excursion hitherto.

"Each time we draw near, they evaporate," Michael shouted, disappointment obvious in his voice. "Maybe they can expect everything we might do."

Rebecca, her temple wrinkled in fixation, contributed, "There should be a hole — a source inside our positions that is warning them."

Sarah's eyes enlarged with concern. "Yet, who could we at any point trust?" she asked, her voice touched with disquiet.

The room fell into quiet, the heaviness of their problem weighty upon them. The mystery society's impact appeared to stretch out even to the spots they had once viewed as protected.

All of a sudden, a thump on the entryway ended the quiet. Michael mindfully moved toward the entryway, his hand laying on his weapon. He opened it to find Sinclair remaining there, a grave demeanor all over.

"I trust I'm not intruding on," Sinclair said, his voice touched with lament. "I heard your disappointment and figured I could possibly help."

Michael looked at Sinclair watchfully, yet after a second, he moved to one side to give him access. Sinclair had demonstrated his devotion during their fight against the mysterious society, yet the past was not effortlessly neglected.

"I get it on the off chance that you have no faith in me totally," Sinclair said, recognizing the obvious issue at hand. "Be that as it may, I need to offer to set things straight for my past. I can't change what I've done, yet I can help you now."

Rebecca, ever the practical person, saw an open door. "What could you at any point offer?" she asked, her look fixed on Sinclair.

"I know how their activities work," Sinclair answered. "I can assist you with exploring the maze, uncover the holes, lastly deal with them."

Sarah took a gander at Sinclair, her heart conflicted between uncertainty and the longing to have confidence in recovery. "Might we at any point trust you?" she asked, her voice loaded up with weakness.

"I won't imagine that my past doesn't torment me," Sinclair conceded. "In any case, I need to make things right. I need to assist you with stopping this haziness."

Michael, his analyst impulses directing his judgment, concentrated on Sinclair intently. He could detect the authentic regret as would be natural for Sinclair, and he knew that occasionally, reclamation came from the unlikeliest of spots.

After a snapshot of thought, Michael at long last gestured. "Okay, Sinclair," he said, expanding his hand. "We'll allow you an opportunity to show what you can do."

Sinclair shook Michael's hand solidly, appreciation obvious in his eyes. "Much obliged to you," he said essentially.

With Sinclair's information and newly discovered assurance, the partners set out on a restored quest for the mysterious society. Their joint effort carried them nearer to the subtle path, and they started to destroy the releases that had prevented their advancement.

As they followed the maze of double dealing, the shadows of the past appeared to withdraw, inch by inch. The excess individuals from the mysterious society were uncovered, and with every disclosure, a fair consequence was given.

However, the maze had one last curve — a disclosure that deeply impacted the partners. The genuine brains behind the mysterious society, the one calling the shots from the shadows, was somebody they had never thought — a figure of power whose impact stretched out a long way above and beyond.

In the climactic showdown, the partners dealt with the genius directly, the heaviness of their excursion and the recollections of their fallen confidants powering their assurance. Reality at long last arisen, enlightening the most obscure corners of the maze.

As the last pieces made sense, the partners dealt with the genius, presenting their deeds to the radiance of day. The city, indeed, inhaled a moan of help, realizing that the last remnants of defilement had been destroyed.

In the repercussions of their triumph, the partners stood joined together, their bonds more grounded than at any other time. The shadows of the past had at long last been thrown away, supplanted by a recharged feeling of trust and a city on the way to genuine mending.

As London luxuriated in the beginning of another day, Michael, Sarah, Rebecca, and Sinclair realize that their process was not even close to finished. In any case, with equity winning and reclamation found in unforeseen spots, they were prepared to confront anything challenges lay ahead. For in the core of the city, the unstoppable soul of its kin and the force of solidarity had won over even the most obscure of mazes.

Chapter 23: Echoes of the past

As the residue chose the last a conflict with the mystery society's brains, London inhaled a deep breath of help. The city was recuperating, and equity had beaten murkiness. Michael Craig, Sarah, Rebecca, and Sinclair had arisen as the heroes of individuals, their purpose and solidarity rousing a freshly discovered trust in the hearts of Londoners.

Yet, even directly following triumph, the reverberations of the past waited. The scars left by the mystery society's debasement ran profound, and the partners realize that their work was nowhere near finished. As they stood together, looking out over the city they had battled to safeguard, they shared a snapshot of reflection.

"We've made considerable progress," Michael pondered, ending the quiet that wrapped them. "Be that as it may, there's still a lot to be finished."

Sarah gestured in understanding; her heart still weighty with the heaviness of the mysteries they had uncovered. "The injuries of the past will find opportunity to recuperate," she said delicately. "In any case, we have one another, and that makes the biggest difference."

Rebecca, ever the realist, contributed, "We want to guarantee that the changes we've set up stay in one piece. The general public's impact might be gone, however there will continuously be the people who look to take advantage of the powerless."

Sinclair, who played had a surprising influence in their triumph, added, "I'll give my best for help. I owe it to London and to every one of the people who endured in view of the general public's debasement."

With their common perspective revived, the partners realize that their process was not yet at an end. They got back to their separate jobs — Michael proceeding with his analyst work, Sarah offering help to those out of luck, Rebecca regulating the city's changes, and Sinclair attempting to set things straight for his past.

In the days that followed, London went through a change. The once-shadowed roads started to load up with life and light, a demonstration of the flexibility of its kin. The scars of defilement started to recuperate, and a newly discovered feeling of trust and solidarity saturated the city.

Nonetheless, as the partners before long found, leftovers of the mysterious society persevered as another danger — one that was more treacherous and trickier than any other time in recent memory. Gossipy tidbits about a strange figure, referred to just as "The Ghost," started to flow. Murmurs of undercover gatherings and plots to weaken the city consumed the atmosphere.

Michael, ever the sharp, not entirely set in stone to make quick work of this new threat. Yet again with Sarah and Rebecca next to him, he dug into the shadows, looking for hints that would lead them to The Ghost's refuge.

Their examination drove them to the most obscure corners of London — the underground passages and secret entries that had once filled in as the mystery society's space. As they explored the maze of trickery, they experienced old partners and enemies the same, each with their own plan and insider facts to secure.

Amidst their interest, the partners coincidentally found a startling partner — a previous individual from the mysterious society, who had become frustrated with its vindictive ways. This insider furnished them with significant data, directing them nearer to The Apparition's actual personality.

As they surrounded their quarry, the reverberations of the past appeared to become stronger. The recollections of their fallen confidants and the penances made in their quest for equity reemerged, driving them forward in their assurance to safeguard London.

At long last, the partners cornered The Ghost, and reality behind the perplexing figure was uncovered. The Ghost ended up being a previous partner of the mysterious society — a splendid controller who had quickly jumped all over the chance to ascend to drive following the general public's defeat.

The showdown that followed was serious, with The Apparition utilizing each stunt available to them to avoid catch. Yet, Michael, Sarah, Rebecca, and Sinclair ended up being a relentless power, their solidarity and resolve a conspicuous difference to The Ghost's frantic endeavors to keep up with control.

Eventually, The Apparition's snare of trickiness unwound, and they were dealt with. London by and by inhaled a murmur of help, thankful for the partners' faithful obligation to safeguard the city from the shadows that took steps to overwhelm it.

As the reverberations of the past leisurely blurred, another part started for London. The city remained as a demonstration of the unstoppable soul of its kin and the force of solidarity despite haziness. The partners had confronted their own evil presences and had arisen more grounded, prepared to confront anything challenges lay ahead.

In the core of London, the reverberations of their victory resonated, motivating expectation in the hearts of all who called the city home. As the sun set on their most recent triumph, Michael, Sarah, Rebecca, and Sinclair realize that their process would proceed, for the way to equity was a ceaseless one. Yet, together, they were ready to confront anything shadows what was in store held, secure in the information that their solidarity and love would constantly light the way.

Section 24: Another Dawn

In the consequence of their victory over The Ghost, London remained on the slope of another sunrise. The reverberations of the past had blurred, supplanted by a restored feeling of trust and solidarity. Michael Craig, Sarah, Rebecca, and Sinclair ended up at an intersection — their common process against debasement had manufactured a strong bond, yet the opportunity had arrived for them to confront their own fates.

As the city lounged toward the beginning of the day light, Michael and Sarah stood together on the housetop of their safehouse, looking out at the enlivening roads underneath. The city's heart beat with life, but, there was a tranquil serenity in the air — a break after the determined quest for equity.

"You know," Michael started, ending the quiet, "it's been a long excursion for us."

Sarah gestured, her hand laced with Michael's. "Indeed, yet it's an excursion I wouldn't change for anything," she answered, her eyes mirroring the affection they had shared through the hardships.

"We've confronted obscurity together and arisen more grounded," Michael proceeded, "and I can't envision a future without you close by."

Sarah grinned, her heart loaded up with appreciation for the one who had remained by her all through everything.

"Furthermore, I can't envision a future without you possibly," she said. "We've confronted such a ton together, and I know that together, we can confront whatever comes straightaway."

As they remained there, their adoration and solidarity fortified, the heaviness of their process started to lift. They realize that the scars of their past could never completely blur, however they were prepared to embrace a fresh start — a future based on the groundwork of trust, love, and equity.

In the interim, Rebecca dove into the city's changes, guaranteeing that the progressions they had contended energetically to execute stayed in one piece. Her essential psyche and empathetic heart directed her as she explored the complexities of administration, always remembering individuals whose lives had been moved by debasement.

Sinclair, as well, tracked down a reason past his past. He looked for recovery by devoting himself to aiding those impacted by the mystery society's deeds. His reconstruction enlivened other people who had once strolled a hazier way, demonstrating that the force of progress and reclamation was inside everybody's grip.

As the days went to weeks, the partners started to float towards their singular reasons for living. Be that as it may, the bond they had produced during their common process stayed tough. They kept on get-together at their safehouse, sharing their victories and difficulties, realizing that they were more grounded together than separated.

Yet again one night, as the sun set over the city, projecting tones of orange and gold over the roads, the partners wound up accumulated at their safehouse. The room was loaded up with a feeling of wistfulness, as they pondered their excursion from outsiders united by situation to a unified power battling for equity.

"We've made considerable progress," Rebecca said, a sprinkle of feeling in her voice. "I could never have requested better partners."

"Nor could I," Sinclair concurred, thankful for the additional opportunity he had been given.

Sarah glanced around at her friends, her heart loaded up with affection and pride. "I'm pleased with all we've achieved together," she said. "Furthermore, I'm appreciative for all of you."

Michael gestured, his eyes meeting Sarah's, a quiet confirmation of their unfaltering adoration. "We've confronted our own evil presences and vanquished them," he said. "Together, we've made London a superior spot."

As they sat together, sharing stories and chuckling, they realize that the excursion against debasement would proceed. New difficulties would emerge, yet they were ready to confront them with the strength of their solidarity and the recollections of their common victories.

In the weeks that followed, Michael, Sarah, Rebecca, and Sinclair left on their singular ways, secure in the information that they would constantly be partners in the battle for equity. London kept on modifying, embracing another time of straightforwardness and sympathy, and the reverberations of the past were overwhelmed by the aggregate any expectation of a more promising time to come.

In the core of the city, the partners' heritage persevered — a demonstration of the dauntless soul of its kin and the force of adoration, equity, and solidarity even with obscurity. Their process had molded them, making a permanent imprint on their souls and brains, and as they looked towards the skyline, they realized that anything challenges lay ahead, they would confront them as one.

Thus, as the sun rose on another day, projecting its warm light over the city, London stood prepared to confront anything that what was to come held — a city recuperated by the boldness of its kin and the information that, eventually, it was the force of solidarity and love that had prevailed over even the most obscure of shadows.

Chapter 25: Uninvited Guests

Directly following their triumph, London relaxed in the sparkle of another day break, its roads loaded up with a feeling of restoration and trust. Michael Craig, Sarah, Rebecca, and Sinclair had become neighborhood legends — their names murmured in stunningness by the people who had seen the city's change. In any case, as the days transformed into weeks, another test lingered not too far off — one that would test the partners' solidarity and assurance more than ever.

One night, as the partners accumulated at their safehouse, a feeling of kinship and satisfaction occupied the room. The glow of a snapping chimney encompassed them, its moving flares creating glimmering shaded areas on the walls.

"I can't really accept that how far we've come," Rebecca commented, a little grin playing all the rage.

Sinclair gestured, his eyes mirroring the appreciation he felt. "I owe you for my entire life," he expressed, checking out at every one of them thusly. "Without your trust and confidence in me, I'd in any case be caught in the obscurity."

Sarah connected and put a consoling hand on Sinclair's shoulder. "We as a whole have our pasts," she said, her voice delicate. "In any case, what is important is our decisions now and individuals we've become."

As the discussion proceeded, their feeling of solidarity just developed further. They had confronted dimness together and arisen successful, a demonstration of the force of affection, equity, and solidarity. In any case, as the night wore on, a thump on the entryway intruded on their tranquility.

Michael, ever the careful criminal investigator, rose up to respond to it. He made the way for track down an unforeseen visitor — an old man, slight and shaking, his face concealed underneath the folds of a worn-out coat.

"Might I at any point help you?" Michael asked, his analyst senses on guard.

The man's voice was dry, as though it hadn't been utilized in years. "I've come to look for your guide," he said, his words scarcely discernible.

Moving to one side, Michael welcomed the man in. The partners assembled around him, a combination of interest and worry in their eyes.

"I'm Reginald Everard," the man said, at long last uncovering his face. His eyes were loaded up with a profound exhaustion that appeared to rise above time. "I was once an individual from the mysterious society — the extremely one you battled against."

The room fell quiet, the heaviness of Reginald's disclosure settling upon them like a weighty haze.

"Yet, I've since a long time ago left their positions," Reginald, his voice trembled. "I became baffled with their noxiousness, and I needed out. They swore they'd kill me in the event that I at any point left, yet I needed to get away."

Sarah's heart went out to the man before her, perceiving the trepidation and agony that he conveyed with him. "Why have you come to us?" she asked tenderly.

"I've been living sequestered from everything, attempting to get away from their grip," Reginald made sense of. "Yet, presently, I dread they're surrounding me. I know excessively, and they won't rest until I'm hushed."

Michael's brain dashed, sorting out the data. "Assuming they're coming after you," he said, "it implies there's something they actually need to stow away."

Reginald gestured. "There's confidential — an old curio that they've been looking for quite a long time," he uncovered. "It's said to hold enormous power, and they'll remain determined to have it."

The partners traded looks, understanding that their fight against the mysterious society was not even close to finished. The shadows of the past actually waited, and the subtle path they had followed appeared to wander aimlessly again.

"We can't allow them to get their hands on that relic," Sinclair expressed, assurance in his voice. "We've contended energetically to allow them to dive London back into haziness."

Michael concurred, his analyst mind as of now working. "We want to find the antiquity before they do," he said. "Furthermore, we really want to shield Reginald from their grip."

As they examined their following stages, a feeling of direction settled upon them. The slippery path they had followed during their past fight had not genuinely reached a conclusion — it had only taken an alternate structure.

In the days that followed, the partners dug into the secret of the antique. They followed mysterious hints and antiquated texts, looking to unwind its real essence and the risk it presented. With Reginald's assistance, they uncovered a path that drove them to the core of London — a secret chamber underneath the city, where the curio was supposed to be covered up.

As they moved toward the chamber, a feeling of premonition consumed the space. The partners realize that their best course of action would be their generally dangerous yet.

In any case, they were undaunted.

Together, they wandered into the profundities, the shadows of the past apparently merging around them. They confronted traps and hindrances intended to safeguard the antiquity, however their solidarity and assurance demonstrated unflinching.

At long last, they remained before the relic — a glorious and strong item that appeared to murmur with energy. Obviously, the mysterious society had looked for it for its vindictive purposes, and the partners realize that they couldn't permit that to occur.

In a mental breakthrough, Reginald ventured forward. "I might have once been a piece of the haziness," he said, "however I need to assist with fixing things. I'll remain here and gatekeeper the antique. I realize the mysterious society won't rest until they track down it, and I won't allow them to succeed."

His words filled the partners with appreciation and reverence. Reginald had decided to confront his past and track down reclamation in safeguarding the very antiquity he had once tried to have.

With a mutual perspective, Michael, Sarah, Rebecca, and Sinclair promised to safeguard Reginald and guarantee that the relic stayed stowed away from the mystery society's grip.

As they rose up out of the profundities, they realize that the fight against haziness was not even close to finished. However, they were joined together, their purpose reinforced by the information that they would confront the shadows of the past together.

Yet again in the core of London, the reverberations of their victory resonated, a demonstration of the unstoppable soul of its kin and the force of solidarity and love despite murkiness. The partners had confronted their own devils and arisen successful, prepared to confront anything challenges lay ahead.

Thus, as the sun set on one more day, projecting its warm light over the city, London stood watchful against the excluded visitor — the haziness that tried to attack its heart. What's more, with the partners' solidarity as its safeguard, the city stayed ready to confront anything shadows what was in store held, secure in the information that their adoration and equity would continuously light the way.

Chapter 26: Legacy of light

As the days transformed into weeks, the partners stayed careful, protecting the old relic and watching out for the shadows that lingered over London. Reginald Everard, their unforeseen partner, had turned into the caretaker of the antiquity, and he took his obligation to safeguard it with relentless determination. The partners, thus, proceeded with their examination concerning the leftovers of the, not entirely set in stone to guarantee that its haziness could at absolutely no point in the future pollutant the city they cherished.

In their quest for equity, Michael Craig, Sarah, Rebecca, and Sinclair ended up brought into a snare of interest and misleading. The mystery society's impact had run profound, and its ringlets expanded farther than they had at any point expected. In any case, with each lead they followed, they found that their solidarity and assurance could endure even the most imposing difficulties.

As London kept on remaking, the city's kin focused on the partners with reverence and appreciation. Their names had become inseparable from trust and equity, and their heritage was scratched in the core of the city. Yet, even in the midst of the awards, the partners stayed unassuming, realizing that the fight against haziness was a continuous excursion — one that necessary watchfulness and commitment.

Yet again one morning, as the sun cast a brilliant sparkle over the city, the partners accumulated at their safehouse. Their bond had just developed further, their common encounters having manufactured a tough association. Yet, in the midst of the fellowship, there was a feeling of vulnerability in the air — an acknowledgment that their excursion, as a unified power, could before long reach a conclusion.

"London is recuperating," Rebecca said, her look floating through the window to the clamoring roads beneath. "Furthermore, we had an impact in that recuperating."

Sinclair gestured, a feeling of satisfaction in his eyes. "We've had an effect," he said. "We've carried light to the shadows."

Sarah grinned; her heart loaded with affection for the partners who had turned into her loved ones. "I'm thankful for every one of you," she said. "You've given me the solidarity to confront my past and embrace what's in store."

Michael, ever the indifferent investigator, shouted out. "Our process isn't finished," he said. "In any case, we might have to follow various ways from here."

The room fell into insightful quietness. The partners realize that their predeterminations were entwined, however they likewise realize that they had their own fights to take on — conflicts that were profoundly private and required individual determination.

As the day went to nightfall, the partners wound up remaining on the housetop of their safehouse, looking out at the city that had been the background of their common process. The sun plunged beneath the skyline, projecting tints of orange and gold over the city, and the lights of London started to sparkle like stars in the night sky.

"We'll continuously be partners," Sarah said, ending the quietness. "Regardless of where our ways take us."

Michael gestured, his eyes mirroring the adoration he felt for every one of them. "That is a commitment," he said. "We'll continuously be partners, limited by our mutual perspective and our adoration for this city."

As the night wore on, the partners earnestly committed to an unbreakable promise — to safeguard London and its kin, to carry light to the shadows, and to continuously stand joined even with obscurity.

In the weeks that followed, the partners followed their own ways, each committing themselves to a reason they put stock in. Michael proceeded with his criminal investigator work, carrying equity to the people who looked to hurt the guiltless. Sarah utilized her sympathy to help the defenseless, giving guide and backing to those out of luck. Rebecca zeroed in on administration, guaranteeing that the city's changes stayed in salvageable shape and that a fair consequence was given without predisposition. Sinclair, as well, proceeded with his quest for reclamation, helping those impacted by the dimness he had once been a piece of.

Yet, even as they left on their singular processes, their bond stayed tough. The partners kept on social affair at their safehouse, sharing their victories and difficulties, and it were never genuinely alone to remind each other that they.

As the years passed, their names became legends in the chronicles of London's set of experiences. Their tradition of light and equity had made a permanent imprint on the city, motivating people in the future to emulate their example. The partners' story was recapped in books and stories, a sign of the force of solidarity, love, and equity despite murkiness.

Thus, as the sun set on London one last time, projecting its warm light over the city, the reverberations of the partners' victory resonated — a demonstration of the unyielding soul of its kin and the tradition of light that they had abandoned. For in the core of the city, the partners' bond persevered, an encouraging sign for all who confronted the shadows of the past and the difficulties representing things to come. The excursion against murkiness would proceed, yet with the tradition of the partners to direct them, London would perpetually remain steadfast, washed in the radiance of equity and love.

The End

Epilogue: An Immortal Heritage

Years had passed since the partners' victorious triumph over dimness, however their heritage got through like a timeless fire, projecting its gleam over London for a long time into the future.

The city had changed, miraculously rising like a phoenix after debasement and embracing a future based on equity, solidarity, and sympathy. The scars of the past had blurred, supplanted by a feeling of versatility and trust that pervaded each road and rear entryway.

The tales of Michael Craig, Sarah, Rebecca, and Sinclair had become woven into the texture of London's set of experiences. Their names were spoken with veneration, their activities deified in sculptures and works of art. They had become legends, their deeds motivating new ages to battle for equity and to stand joined notwithstanding murkiness.

In the core of the city, the safehouse that had once been the partners' safe-haven had turned into an image of trust — where the exhausted and discouraged tracked down comfort and backing. It had changed into a shelter for those looking for equity, its walls reverberating with the tradition of the unyielding triplet and their surprising partner.

Michael, presently a carefully prepared analyst, had resigned from well-trained however kept on offering his direction and mastery to the up-and-coming age of examiners.

His sharp eye and enduring feeling of equity had turned into a reference point for the people who looked to emulate his example.

Sarah had turned into a mainstay of sympathy and recuperating, her graciousness and compassion contacting the existences of incalculable spirits. She had laid out havens and backing places for the defenseless, guaranteeing that nobody in London would be abandoned.

Rebecca had proceeded with her work in administration, her essential psyche and faithful honesty forming the city's future. Her changes had turned into a foundation of London's flourishing, and her vision had changed the city into a stronghold of reasonableness and opportunity.

Sinclair, when a man tormented by haziness, had tracked down recovery in his devotion to helping other people. He had turned into a guide to those looking to get away from the grip of defilement, his own process filling in as a demonstration of the force of progress and the strength of the human soul.

The safehouse, presently an image of trust and solidarity, remained as a demonstration of the partners' heritage. It had turned into a position of journey for those looking for motivation, and guests from varying backgrounds came to offer their appreciation to the legends who had once called it home.

As the years transformed into hundreds of years, the reverberations of the partners' victory kept on resounding through the ages. Their story had turned into a piece of London's fables, passed down starting with one age then onto the next, an update that notwithstanding haziness, the force of affection, equity, and solidarity could win.

Thus, as the sun set on London, projecting its warm light over the city, the tradition of the partners persevered. Their names might have been failed to remember by some, however their soul lived on in each thoughtful gesture, in each quest for equity, and in each hand reached out to those out of luck.

For in the core of London, the tradition of Michael Craig, Sarah, Rebecca, and Sinclair sparkled like a signal, directing the city through the ages and reminding its kin that, eventually, the radiance of equity and love would constantly win over the most obscure of shadows.

Don't miss out!

Visit the website below and you can sign up to receive emails whenever M Safee publishes a new book. There's no charge and no obligation.

https://books2read.com/r/B-A-ODHZ-BDXLC

BOOKS 2 READ

Connecting independent readers to independent writers.